Hidden in the Hollow

By

Ronna M. Bacon

Verses

2 Samuel 22:3 My God is my rock, in whom I take refuge, my shield and the horn of my salvation. He is my stronghold, my refuge and my savior— from violent people you save me. 4 "I called to the LORD, who is worthy of praise, and have been saved from my enemies.

Psalm 121:1 I lift up my eyes to the mountains— where does my help come from? 2 My help comes from the LORD, the Maker of heaven and earth.

Table of contents

Dear Readers

Prologue

The young man looked up as he heard the doorbell to his apartment ring and frowned. He wasn't expecting anyone. His young wife would be back shortly, he thought, and she had her own key. He glanced at the computer monitor even as he rose from his chair, glad to have been able to finish off that last paper for the year, sending it to his professor.

He stood, hand on the open door, as he stared at the police officer and the police chaplain standing in front of him, grim looks on their faces. His head began to shake as he heard their words. No, he thought, they're wrong. She'll be home in a moment. He stepped outside and looked around them, searching for her.

The chaplain's hand on his shoulder brought his attention back to them. He heard their words but didn't understand. He broke free and ran, heading for the trail he knew she always walked, ignoring the calls from behind him.

The officers guarding the trail tackled him, taking him down, preventing him from going forward. He knew them well, working with them. He shook, his emotions on his face and deep sorrow in his eyes. He sat on the bumper of a truck, friends on either side, as his eyes were trained down the trail, looking in vain for her. She didn't appear. Instead, he saw the police chief and the medical examiner heading his way. His head dropped, and tears fell as he realized that she would never be coming home again.

He couldn't take in the words they were saying. He finally pushed past them, his eyes on the figure covered with a blanket that he could see. Sobs rose within him as he felt an arm around his shoulders. They had called his brother to come, to be with him.

It's not fair, Lord, he raged, as he paced his apartment after the funeral. We've newlyweds. She's too young to die. They can't tell me what killed her. Why not?

His brother watched, concern on his face, before the young man turned, pointing to the door, asking to be alone. His brother nodded, stopping for a moment to hug him tightly.

The stranger stood across from the old building the apartment was in, gleeful that what he had planned had worked. No one was the wiser, he thought. Good. Now to continue with what he was told to do. Somehow, he didn't think they would ever figure out what had caused her death. That's the way it should be.

Chapter 1

*W*alking across the park towards a picnic table where his friends were waiting on an early spring Saturday, Detective William Buckley was discontented. He had been told to take his accrued vacation, and now he had no idea what to do with his time. Greeting his friends, he dropped his takeout meal bag on the table, then slid into a seat, his eyes searching for something, anything that would break up the monotony of the next thirty days off. It's only the first day, Lord, and I'm bored already. I guess You're telling me I need a life?

Faith and Josiah Silverthorn exchanged concerned glances with her cousin, Noah Lockwood, and his wife, Rowan. They knew Bill had been working a lot of overtime, but hadn't realized how close to the edge he had gotten.

"Bill?" Noah's voice cut through his Bill's thoughts and he brought his attention back to his friends.

"Sorry, guys." He shrugged, even as he grinned at them.

"Not a problem, but it would be nice if you stayed with us." Faith shook her finger at her long-time friend.

"I'll try, Faith, but you know how hard it is for me to concentrate on simple things sometimes." He looked up as he heard footsteps on the path behind Faith and Josiah and frowned.

Faith turned, then jumped from her seat, approaching the woman walking rapidly towards them.

"Coretta?" Faith stopped, her eyes on the woman, knowing she was a friend from school. She hadn't seen her in years.

"Faith? Hi!" Cora, as she was known, stopped, her eyes searching Faith's face and then lifting to look around.

"It's good to see you. Can you join us?" Faith nodded towards the table where the others were sitting.

"I'm sorry, Faith. Not today." Cora moved to walk by her, but Faith's hand on her arm stopped her.

"Just for a moment? I'd like you to meet my Josiah. Noah would like to say hi as well."

Cora struggled within herself to overcome the sudden sense of fear she felt, finally nodding. "Just not too long. I have things I need to be getting to."

Faith frowned as she turned, seeing the haunted look in Cora's face and feeling the stress emanating from her. *This is not my friend, Lord. What happened to her?*

Josiah, Noah and Bill all rose to their feet as the two women approached.

"Josiah, this is my friend, Cora Brodie. You've heard me speak of her. Cora, my husband, Josiah. You know Noah, of course. That's his wife, Rowan." She watched as Cora greeted them, reserve on her face. "And you remember Bill Buckley."

Cora turned, her hazel eyes searching Bill's face, recognizing the friend from years past.

"It's Weston." Cora's voice was quiet as she spoke.

"I'm sorry. Cora?" Faith turned to her, a puzzled look on her face.

"My name's Weston now, Cora." She nodded at the group and then excused herself.

Faith sank down on the seat, her eyes on her friend, troubled by the abrupt way Cora had left. "That's not the Cora I remember." She looked over at Noah. "Did you know she was married?"

Noah nodded. "I did. You hadn't heard?" When Faith shook her head, Noah exchanged a glance with Bill, who was watching the cousins, an unreadable look on his face. "She was married a year ago, a year from today actually."

"Then, where's her husband?"

"He was killed just as they were leaving the church. You really didn't know that?" Noah's voice had a trace of rebuke for his cousin. "You two were so close."

"We were, but I lost touch with her. Oh, Noah! No wonder she didn't want to stop and talk." Faith spun on her seat, searching for her friend. "Bill?" She turned to him, to find he was no longer seating there. "Now, where'd he go?"

Bill walked rapidly after Cora, his eyes searching the area around him as a matter of habit. His steps slowed as he saw her leaning against the railing overlooking the short drop-off to the river. He stopped beside her, his hands grasping the metal railing.

She finally spoke. "Why'd you come after me, Bill?"

He shrugged. "You're my friend. I haven't seen you in years, but I would like to just be there for you."

She turned, anger burning in her glance before it faded to extreme pain and anguish. "You know, don't you?"

He nodded, his dark blue eyes assessing her. "I heard. I'm a police officer, Cora. I was working on a case with that city's police department near the church last year and heard the call. I didn't know at the time it was you." He brushed back the black hair that had fallen over his brow.

She gave an abrupt nod, her hand pulling at the dark brown curls she had pulled back into a pony tail. "It was. It hurts, Bill. We were planning on moving back here. I'm only here long enough to help Mom sort out Uncle John's stuff."

Bill nodded again. "I hear what you're saying. I lost my wife just as we were married six months." He swallowed hard, not able to continue.

"I didn't know you had married, Bill."

He shrugged. "I had." He turned as he heard running footsteps and then flew over the railing with a loud cry. He heard Cora scream beside him and then he had landed hard, blackness closing in on him.

Cora's body lay beside him, neither moving as onlookers raced to the railing and then moved aside as Josiah and Noah were there, quickly scaling the railing and dropping the ten feet or so to the ground below. Josiah hit the dirt, his hands reaching to assess Bill even as Noah checked on Cora. Noah looked up, nodding at the question Rowan was calling to him. Faith's focus was on the two men running from the scene. She frowned, thinking that they looked familiar, but she couldn't place them.

Chapter 2

$\mathscr{P}$olice Chief Andrew McBeth stood near the doors of the ambulance as he watched Bill being assessed by the paramedics. He smiled as he heard the argument going on and knew Bill would win. He wouldn't be going to the hospital.

He turned as a patrol officer approached, moving away to speak with him, his eyes raising to where Cora sat on a bench, Faith beside her, before nodding and moving her way.

"Mrs. Weston?" Andrew felt he was being too formal, but he didn't know the lady.

"Chief?" Cora's eyes narrowed as she studied Andrew, before she sighed. "I have no idea who it was. I'm not staying in this town, if you're worried that I brought trouble with me."

"Not at all. I'm just concerned that you're okay. Did you get yourself checked out?"

Cora nodded. "I'm fine. I've taken a lot longer and harder falls than that one." She stood, ignoring the question on his face at her statement. "Have you any more questions? If not, I have an appointment I need to get to."

Andrew shook his head, watching as she strode away. Faith rose to stand beside him.

"I'm sorry, Andrew. She's different than she used to be."

"Understandably, given what she's gone through. I hear she had a real tragedy." Andrew turned as Bill approached.

"She did. I never knew until Noah mentioned it. We had lost touch. I see her mother but she never mentioned anything."

Bill stood by Andrew. "She's grieving, Faith. She lost a huge part of who she was and what her life would be like when her husband was killed. And it was a nasty episode. He bled out in her arms from the stab wound. The man had headed for Cora but Nigel stepped into the way." Bill's eyes were shadowed as he stared into the distance where he could still see Cora.

Andrew studied his friend. "You okay, Bill?"

Bill gave an abrupt nod. "Seeing how Cora is hurting brings back some real painful memories for me, that's all." His eyes grew shadowed as a shuttered look came over his face. "It reminds too much of when I lost Elizabeth."

"Elizabeth?" Andrew and Faith shared a questioning look.

Bill nodded, not even really seeing their looks. "My wife. I lost her when we were only married for six months." With that, he walked away, leaving the two staring open mouthed after him.

"Andrew? Did you know?"

Andrew shook his head at Faith's quiet question. "Never. He has never ever said a word until now." He turned to watch her face, his eyes lifting as he saw Josiah standing behind her. "He keeps his personal life very close to himself, Faith. He always has. I've known him for years and never knew this. It would have been when they were in college, before he joined the force."

Faith shook her head. "I still feel bad, Andrew. We were part of such a close group of friends during high school. Now we've drifted apart. I don't like it."

"You don't have to like it, Faith." Josiah hugged his wife from behind. "It's Bill's private life. If he wants to talk about it now, he will. Otherwise, we don't pry. The same with Cora. Call on her in a couple of days and see if she's have coffee or lunch with you while she's here."

Bill turned as Andrew walked across his back deck towards him, handing over a cup of coffee. Bill sighed. He knew he had to talk with Andrew at some point, but some days the emotions were too raw. Today was one of them. Lord, I thought I had moved on, that everything was under control. Today proved otherwise.

Andrew didn't speak, sipping at his coffee, waiting for Bill to talk. His heart was burdened for his friend and he did the only thing he knew how to do. He prayed for his friend.

"Thanks, Andrew." Bill finally spoke.

"For what?" Andrew turned to face his friend.

"For not making a big deal today with Faith. She would have kept digging at it."

Andrew snorted. "She would have. I'm here whenever you want to talk."

Bill nodded, finally sighing. "I've never told anyone I've worked with. Wesley knows, of course." He spoke of his younger brother. "Most days I'm fine. But days like this, seeing how much a friend is hurting. It brings it all back."

"Do you want to talk about it?"

Bill finally nodded, swiping at the tears on his cheeks. "We met our first day at college. We married after we finished our junior year. She was going to set up her own business of helping the less fortunate navigate government bureaucracy. Two weeks before Christmas, I got a knock at my door, finding an officer and the chaplain standing there, telling that they had found her on the walking trail she loved to walk. No visible signs of injuries. No medical reason for death. The coroner described it as if she had been so terrified her body just shut down. There was absolutely no evidence of anything, Andrew." He nodded at a file folder sitting on the table. "I made you a copy of what I've done over the years. I know she was scared of something or someone, that something had happened about a month before that. We never could figure out who it was. We both looked. The police looked. No one was ever found." He looked up at that point, to find Andrew watching him, compassion in his gaze. "You know the drill. Every year, they call just to check in, just to tell me they haven't found anything."

"I'll look into it, Bill, and see if fresh eyes can come up with something. I'll pass it on to Emma at Tracker's as well if that's okay."

Bill nodded. "She's already looked into it some for me. I think I need to push it now. It's time."

Andrew hesitated, not knowing how to continue. "Are you sure, Bill?"

Bill turned back to face Andrew. "I'm sure. I need to move on, if I can, and I can't while this is still there." He paused, his eyes on the fingers he was rubbing together. "Seeing Cora today, seeing how a friend is hurting. Yeah, it's time." He looked up. "I'll leave it with you, Andrew. Whatever you need or it takes, please do what you can." With a quiet goodbye, he walked off the deck and around to where he had parked.

Andrew stared after him, finally reaching for the folder. Knowing Bill as well as he did, there would be as many facts and names as Bill could find. He opened it and then headed into his home office. It was going to be a late night, he knew.

Chapter 3

*C*ora walked into the church, feeling uncomfortable as she did so. It had been a year since she had last attended church. She felt that God had abandoned her, hadn't listened to her pleas for Nigel's life as she had held him, sobbing, crying out to God to save him. But she also couldn't not go, given the look on her mother's face. She wouldn't sit with her parents, though. They sat too far forward. She looked around, not really seeing anyone she knew. She jumped as a voice spoke beside her.

"Cora?" Bill stood, watching her.

"Bill! You scared me." Her hand was at her throat.

"Sorry!" He grinned at her. "Where were you planning on sitting?"

She shook her head. "I'm not sure where. I don't want to sit near the front. This is hard enough as it is."

He nodded to a back pew. "How about there? It's where I usually sit."

She sighed, finally moving to where he had indicated. "Don't be surprised if I leave halfway through."

He shrugged. "And I'll go with you."

She stared at him, then turned her attention to the front of the church. "That's a new minister."

"Silas? He's been here ten years or so. He's a good friend of mine."

She nodded, then sat quiet. Bill could feel the tension growing within and knew she wouldn't last the service. He frowned as he felt eyes watching him. He turned, searching, knowing the feeling, but couldn't see anyone.

Partway through the service, Cora began to shake. She clenched her hands together but couldn't stop. Her face paled and she had difficulty breathing. Bill gave a small sound, then arm around her, swept her from the pew and outside to his car.

"Did you drive today?" When Cora shook her head, he opened the door and stuffed her inside, running around to slide behind the wheel. "Where would you like to go, Cora?"

She shook her head, not able to speak for the tears blocking her throat. Bill studied her for a moment, then pulled from the parking lot, heading for a spot on the river where they had spent many days with their friends. He reached for her hand and led her to the rocks, seating her, then sitting beside her, not saying anything.

She swiped at the tears and took the handkerchief he held out for her. She studied it before looking up at him.

"Cloth, Bill?"

He grinned as he nodded. "Elizabeth got me started on that. I just kept it up."

"Does it get any easier?" Her eyes searched his.

He shrugged. "In some ways it does. In other ways it doesn't. It's been ten years for me, Cora. It still hurts." He paused, staring out over the river. "Elizabeth would have wanted me to move on, to find someone to share my life with. I just haven't had the heart."

She nodded. "Nigel and I spoke about that. I know he would want that for me, but I'm not sure I'll ever be ready."

"When or if. The timing is yours, Cora." He looked down at the hands he had clenched together and visibly relaxed them. "I'm not sure if I ever will be."

She sighed. "Mom's after me to move on. She just doesn't get."

He shook his head. "Some don't. I'm sure she has your best interests at heart." He shot a look at her. "Tell me. What have you been up to the last few years?"

"Working. I travel and do videos of my travels. But I want to stop that. It was what Nigel and I had planned to continue. He was trained as a botanist and we'd search out different places for him to research. The desire to travel so much has waned. I met him about three years ago on one of my trips overseas."

Bill nodded. "I understand." He stood, reaching for her hand. "Come on. We need to eat. I know of a place about an hour from here. No one will recognize us, I can guarantee you that."

She studied him for a moment, then shrugged. "Sure, why not?"

Bill seated Cora, then slid into a chair across from her, looking around the restaurant. It was one he frequented on a routine basis, but it was outside of town so he felt it was safe for Cora to be there. He felt the danger she was under.

She looked at him. "You walked out on the service, Bill. You shouldn't have. What will your pastor think?"

He shrugged. "He knows I do what I have to with friends. He understands. He'd have done the same thing."

She shook her head. "I don't understand that thinking. It's not what I have come to expect."

He shrugged once more. "It's who we are, Cora. Now. We eat. Then we talk."

Cora sat back, fear and frustration growing within her. She didn't want to have this conversation, but she knew Bill well enough from the past to know she'd have to.

Bill watched her over the meal, his heart breaking for his friend, his thoughts raised in prayer. He knew she didn't want to do this, but she would.

"Okay, Bill. What do you want to know?" Cora finally looked up at him.

He rose and then tucked her hand into his arm as they walked out. He pointed towards the rose gardens. "Let's walk in there. The roses here are gorgeous in the summer. They have a really nice seating area where we can sit and talk."

Finally seated, Cora looked around, trying to avoid the questions Bill had. She finally sighed.

"All right. What do you want to know?"

He shrugged. "What do you want to tell me? Tell me what you want to and we'll work with that." He hesitated, then continued. "I know the man who stabbed Nigel was high on drugs or that's what the report was, and it was a random stabbing. I don't see that. You were the target, Cora. How come?"

She shivered. "I know I was."

"Do you have any idea why?" Bill studied her face, reading her reluctance to talk. "I just want to help, Cora. Just want to help you solve this and then move on."

Cora sighed, glad to have someone who knew her, someone she could finally talk to, who would understand. "I think it had something to do with some photos I took about two years ago. I had a break-in at my home, but they didn't take anything. They searched very carefully, not leaving much out of place. I don't keep photos on my computer, working off a backup, and I always lock the backups in a safe overnight or when I'm away from home. Older ones are locked in a safety deposit box."

Bill watched intently as she spoke, weighing her words, and knowing she'd give him as much information as she could. "You reported it?"

"For all the good it did. They didn't find any evidence of a break-in. In fact, they seemed to think I had imagined the whole thing."

"You didn't."

Cora shot him a look. "How do you know that?"

"I know you, Cora. You were a good friend during high school. We had many opportunities to talk. I know this spooked you and that it wasn't a figment of your imagination." He turned to her, his eyes searching her face. "What was in the photos?"

She shrugged. "Scenery. Plants. Nigel and I. Nothing that would have caused anyone to come after me."

"Can I see them?" His request caused her head to shoot up as she stared at him.

Finally shrugging, she agreed. "I can get to them. But it would be tomorrow."

"I'm off on vacation for the next four weeks. I have time. If you can go tomorrow, it's fine with me."

She stared at him, not quite sure if he was serious, but decided that he was. "Sure. I should stop at my place and check the mail. I know it's likely piling up."

He nodded, then reached for her hand. "I know you're struggling, Cora, but let me pray with you." He watched closely before he saw her face soften and she agreed.

"I've missed your prayers, Bill. During high school, sometimes they were the only thing that kept me going."

"I didn't know that." Bill's head bent as he prayed for his friend.

They walked slowly back towards the parking lot, Cora's hand tucked into Bill's arm. Neither of them were sure how that happened, but neither moved away. The connection they felt with one another had intensified and grown over the last few hours, shared grief binding them together in a way mere friendship hadn't.

Bill hesitated as he stood at the edge of the parking lot, his eyes on a black car with dark-tinted windows. He was not getting a good feeling from it.

"Cora, let me tuck you in my car quick. I think we have company that neither one of us wants."

She looked stunned. "Did someone find us after all?"

He nodded. "It may be nothing, but I think they have. In you go."

Bill disappeared from her sight, finally sliding into his seat, a small object in his hand that he studied.

"What is that?" Cora's finger pointed to it.

"A tracking device. They must have planted it at the church. I felt like we were being watched."

"So which one of us are they after?"

Bill shrugged. "Either one of us." He reached over to the glove compartment, pulling out an evidence bag and sealing the tracking device inside. "I'll give this to Andrew. I'm not allowed in the department building for a few weeks."

"And what did you do to get yourself banned?" A small grin crossed Cora's face.

"Too much overtime and not enough time off. I've been working on cases involving friends and it has taken its toll."

"Friends?"

He nodded. "Faith and Josiah. Andrew and Phoebe. Noah and Rowan. Silas and Madigan. That just some of them."

Mouth open, she stared at him, before clamping it closed. "What do you mean, cases?"

"They all had what we term as 'adventures', up to kidnappings, assaults, near death." He shot a glance at her, grinning at her expression. "It has made life interesting, to say the least."

"And you, Bill? No adventures like that?"

He shook his head. "Not really. Some I did get caught up into more than others. But I've been one of the team investigating the crimes." He threw a look at her, watching the conflicting emotions on her face. "I haven't had that adventure yet myself and hope I never do."

"I'm in the midst of it, I think, Bill. Somehow, I think you're part of it now."

Chapter 4

*C*ora was reaching with her key towards the lock on her apartment door when Bill's hand came out to stop her. She glanced up at him, seeing the grim look on his face.

"Bill?"

"Someone's tried to break in. See the scratches around the lock." He moved her back from the door and then down to the lobby. "I'm sure those are fresh. Let's call it in."

She shuddered. "I'm being stalked?"

Bill shrugged. "Not necessarily. But someone knows where you live. They want something you have bad enough they'll risk breaking into your place. Your backups are safe?"

She nodded. "They should be." She watched as the responding patrol officer walked towards them, handing Bill her keys.

Bill had a quiet word with the officer, then reached for her hand, leading her after

32

the officer, waiting until the apartment had been cleared.

"Ma'am?" The officer's voice broke through Cora's thoughts and she jumped. "Sorry." He gave her a smile. "If you'd like to come through your apartment and let me know if anything is missing?"

She drew a deep breath and started forward, stopping as Bill laid a hand on her arm and then reached for her hand. She grasped his tight, her thoughts on what she might find. Lord? Are You really here with me? She hadn't prayed in a year but felt she just had to before she entered her home.

She stopped, her hand going to her mouth, her eyes taking in the destruction she saw.

"Cora?" Bill's voice beside her gave her strength to move forward.

"I'll have to straighten up, Officer, before I know if anything's missing."

He nodded. "I have a team on their way over. Give us a couple of hours to go through. I don't expect we'll find much evidence but we'll log what we find." He shared a look with Bill.

Bill turned Cora back to the door. "Let's go find some place to have a coffee or something. I'll bring you back." He handed the officer his card. "Call me if you need me." He had scrawled Cora's phone number on the back of the card.

He shoved her onto a bench seat in a diner and then slid in beside her, despite her protest that he sit on the other side.

"Not today, Cora. Not here." He stared her down. "I need to keep you safe and this is part of how I can. Now, do you still like your peppermint tea and rye toast?"

She stared at him. "How do you remember that? Nigel never could."

He shrugged. "You're my friend. Of course I remember."

She stared at him some more. "Nigel never could remember what I liked. He should have."

Bill nodded. "He should have. Elizabeth and I could remember what the other liked. I miss that." A momentary trace of sadness crossed his face before he pulled out his phone.

"Silas. It's Bill." Bill laughed as Silas commented on him skipping out on church the day before. "I figured you'd seen me. I was helping a friend." Giving Cora a quick look, he continued. "Listen. What are you and Mads up to today on your day off? You're free? Can Mads get access to some cleaning supplies?"

Silas turned to Madigan, his wife, with that question. "She can. What do you need?"

"Cora's place here in Maple Creek was broken into and the crime scene team is going through it. It will be messy after that as well as having had her place tossed. I just thought that if you two were free, between us three we could help her clean up."

Silas quickly agreed. "We'll stop and grab one of Mark's work vans and meet you there. Just text me the address. Give us an hour tops."

Bill tucked his phone away and reached for his coffee mug, stopping as Cora laid a hand on his arm.

"Bill, what was that all about?"

He looked up, sheepish. "I should have asked if it was okay. I'm just so used to stepping in with friends, I never thought. I'm sorry." He reached for his phone to call Silas back.

"Wait a minute! Did you say something about them helping clean up?"

He nodded. "I did. Silas's in-laws have a disaster restoration company. Mads works for them part time. Do you remember Madigan and Mitchell Browne?"

She thought for a moment. "I do, now that you mention them. They're willing to come here, on what you said is their day off, to help?"

He nodded. "It's what we do, Cora. All of us step in to help our friends. No matter the time of day. No matter the circumstances."

She sipped her tea, then set the cup back down. "I feel afraid, Bill. Something is in the apartment that they were looking for. I have no idea what it is."

He squeezed her hand. "I'm glad I'm with you." He pulled out his phone as it chimed. "They're done, so we can head back over."

Two hours later, Silas straightened up from where he had been tying a garbage bag closed and watched Bill. Bill was setting books back on the book shelf and had paused, his finger tracing a photo. Silas walked over and took a look.

"Is that you when you were a teenager?"

Bill looked up and grinned. "It's our group of friends. Faith and Noah are in here. There were about eight of us that hung around together." A reflective look passed over his face and he opened his mouth to continue, then stopped.

"Bill?"

Bill shook his head and turned to set the photo on the shelf, then stopped, noticing the backing on the frame had loosened. As he moved it, a piece of paper fell out. He reached to pick it up, opening it, his hand freezing as he did so.

"Bill?" Silas' quiet voice caught his attention.

"Silas? What's going on?" He held up the piece of paper, shooting a quick glance towards the bedroom where the two women were working. "Cora says she didn't know I was married. Didn't know my wife's name. So why is Elizabeth's name and picture and information tucked away behind a photo in her apartment?"

Silas stared at his friend, stunned at his words. He caught Bill's arm and pushed him out onto the balcony, shutting the patio doors behind him.

"All right, Bill. Talk. You have never ever said anything about being married. Not in all the years I have known you." Silas watched his friend, compassion on his face, concern in his eyes, a prayer rising from his heart.

"It was ten years ago this Christmas that she died. We were college sweethearts, Silas, marrying after our junior year. We were married for about six months. She was killed two weeks before Christmas. We could never figure out who or how or why." Bill blinked, trying to clear his eyes of tears as he stifled sobs rising within him.

Silas' hand rested on Bill's shoulder as he caught a glimpse of Madigan watching through the doors before she motioned she was praying for them. Silas nodded, not quite sure how to proceed.

"What happened, Bill?"

Bill shook his head. "We never knew. That's the thing. We've never been able to close her file, to say it was natural, an accident, murder. We know it wasn't suicide." He looked down at the paper in his hand. "Somehow, Cora's involved in this. I need to call Andrew."

"First, Bill. Are you sure?"

"I am, Silas. I need to know why this information is here." He pulled out his phone.

"Andrew. Hi."

"Bill. You're on vacation. Why are you calling me?" Andrew's voice was quiet but firm.

"I know I am, but I've had something come up. Cora's place was tossed sometime in the last week or so. I'm helping her straighten up and found information on Elizabeth tucked behind a photo. It's not in her handwriting, so I'm guessing it would be Nigel Weston. Can you track anything on him?"

"I can try. Any idea of a date of birth, description?"

Bill gave him the information he had, having seen a photo of Nigel the year before, and Andrew promised to get back to him as soon as he could. Bill folded the paper and tucked away into his wallet, before looking at Silas, a grim look on his face.

"I don't like this, Silas."

"Nor do I. How sure are you that it's his right name?"

Bill stilled, thinking through what Silas had asked. "I'm not sure at all. His death always seemed suspicious. I know the detective who looked into it and he was never satisfied with what they had in evidence." He pulled his phone out as it chimed.

"Andrew?"

"Bill. There is no Nigel Weston. Who was she married to?"

"That's the name she gave me. What is going on?"

"I have no idea. You need to make sure she stays safe. I don't like this, not one bit. I've a call into the detective who investigated the stabbing." Andrew's voice faded away, then came back strong. "You need to get her away from there, Bill. Are you two alone?"

"No, Silas and Mads are here."

"Good. I'll call you again in about an hour."

"I take it that wasn't good news." Silas' hand stopped Bill's forward motions. "Before you say anything, let Andrew find out more facts for you."

Bill nodded. "It will be hard keeping it from her. She was a good friend and knew me well."

An hour later, Madigan stopped beside Silas as he wrapped his arm around her, pulling her close, his eyes on Bill and Cora. She pointed to the two.

"How close of friends are they, any way, Silas? I know they were in a group of good friends as teens."

Silas shrugged. "I have no idea, Madi. No idea. But I think things are going to get very bad for them."

"Silas?"

He shook his head. "We'll talk later." He walked towards Bill. "I think we're about done here, Bill. Anything else we can do?"

He shook his head as he looked at Cora. "Cora, anything more you need them for?"

"I don't think so." She reached to hug both Madigan and Silas. "I can't thank you enough for giving up time on your day off to come and help me."

Madigan shrugged as she shared a look with Bill. "It's what we do, Cora. Friends come first."

Bill watched them walk away, then turned to Cora. "Now, about your photos. Do you have time to collect them from the bank or not?"

She checked her watch. "Let me grab the ones here and we should have time. I have my laptop at Mom's." She paused when he stopped her.

"Let me take them for you, Cora. Let me take the responsibility for getting them out of here."

She stared at him. "You're worried, aren't you?"

"I am. Do you need to take any more clothes or anything with you? If so, we can hide them in a duffel bag or something. No one would ever know."

She thought for a moment. "I can do that. Just be a couple of minutes."

Bill watched her hurry from the room and then sighed. He knew he would have to have that conversation with her, the one he dreaded, the one where he told her what he had found and what Andrew had told him. Andrew had called him back a while ago and the news he had uncovered wasn't good. There was just no record of a Nigel Weston anywhere.

Cora watched Bill's face from where she stood in the hallway. Something's going on, she thought. Lord, I know I haven't been on speaking terms with You lately, and I've been remiss in that. Forgive me. I feel danger heading Bill's way and I want so much to have him protected. Please don't let him get hurt on my behalf.

Bill looked up, a smile on his face as he reached for her bag and then her hand. She stared down at their clasped hands, wonder in her mind and a thawing in her heart. Bill had always been special to her, more so than any of her other friends.

Bill tucked the backups into his jacket pockets and then pointed to the door, quickly moving Cora from the bank to his car and then away. His eyes moved constantly as he searched for a tail. Not seeing one, he breathed a bit easier.

"Where do you want to take these, Cora?"

She shrugged. "I guess I haven't thought that far ahead. I don't like the idea of them being at Mom's."

"How be I take them? I do have a place I can lock them up. If anything, I'll get them to Andrew and he'll lock them up at the department."

She finally nodded. "That sounds good." She turned, her eyes searching his face. "Thank you for your help today, Bill. I

don't think I could have gotten through it
without you."

Chapter 5

*C*ora stared at her laptop, unwilling to close it down, but not willing yet to see the photos of her and Nigel. Bill watched, compassion on his face, as he waited. He had dropped her off the day before at her Mom's, then placed the backups in his safe. She had shown up at his place early that morning, early enough he was just starting his breakfast after his morning run.

"We can leave it for today, if you like, Cora." Bill set her cup of tea beside her before seating himself on the couch near her.

She shook her head, resolutely plugging in the backup and then starting the program to access it. "We need to do this. We need to find out if there is anything there to help."

Bill's hand reached out to still her hands. She looked up at him, seeing a look on his face she didn't understand. She looked at the paper he held out to her.

"Here. Take this. Read it."

She studied it. "Who is this? This Elizabeth?"

"My wife. This was tucked behind the photo of the eight of us friends from high school. I found it. I asked Andrew to look into a name for me."

She paled, her eyes dark in her face. "Not Nigel's? And you couldn't tell me yesterday?" She shoved back her laptop on the coffee table, about to rise.

Bill's hands clamped her arms and chair in place. "I was in shock, Cora. Why would that information be in the back of that picture? I know that's not your handwriting. You wouldn't have denied knowing I was married if you had known. You wouldn't have done that to me."

She searched his face, then paled even more as her eyes slid closed. "Nigel? He did this?"

Bill waited until she looked back at him. "It was Nigel. There has always been a suspicion about his death, as you know. I asked Andrew to run his name." He looked down, swallowing hard, not quite sure how to proceed.

"What aren't you telling me, Bill?"

"There is no one by the name of Nigel Weston that Andrew can find. No record of him anywhere."

Her face flushed with anger and her words had a bite to them. "Of course he existed. I was married to him. I saw his identification, his birth certificate, his passport, his driver's license." She reached for her laptop case. "I keep them right here." She searched, her hand scrabbling through the case. "That's strange. This is where I always keep them. I never take them out of here. Now, where are they?"

"When did you last see them?"

"Three or four weeks, I think. It was well before I came here." She paused, her eyes sliding closed even as her face paled. "Is that what they were after?"

Bill nodded. "I think it was. Whoever it is, I think, is trying to cover their tracks. They were looking for the photos you took of him when they tossed your place. I didn't see any pictures of you two."

"And I had them. I never noticed but then I didn't clean up the living room." She stared at Bill, tears close to the surface of her eyes. "What did I do, Bill? Who did I really marry? And was it even valid? If he didn't exist, then it can't be, can it?"

Bill watched her closely, compassion clouding his judgement. He reached and pulled her into a hug. She clung to him even as shudders ran through her body. Finally sitting back, she stared at her laptop, determination colouring her thinking.

"Let me see if I can find the photos you wanted to see." She searched, pulling photo after photo to a folder on the desktop of her computer. "I think that's them all now." She sat back, her eyes on the last one. "I really don't have that many of him, now do I? I thought I had more."

Bill reach to enlarge the last photo, a frown on his face, studying it intently. Pulling out his phone, he took a picture and then sent it on to Andrew.

"Andrew? It's Bill. I know. I'm not supposed to be bothering you. Listen. I just sent you a picture of Nigel Weston. I know him. Try looking for Scott West. Yeah. That one." He pocketed his phone

"Now what, Bill?"

He shook his head. "I'll do some researching along with Andrew. But first, we need to do something."

"And what would that be?" Cora watched him.

"We need to go back to where you were living. We need to go back through your apartment. How much time did Nigel, or whatever his name was, spend there?"

She shook her head. "Not a lot. He was always too busy." She sighed. "I guess that should have told me something there, shouldn't it? And I never saw his apartment, come to think of it, other than when I cleaned it out. That's just too strange."

"Very." Bill paused, then motioned to his own office. "Let's move in there. I can do some research on my computer and see what I can find out."

She stood, then looked towards the kitchen. "I'm going to make us some lunch, Bill, if that's okay."

He nodded, then watched as she walked away, dejection in her stance. His heart broke for his friend. This was not what he had expected to find, not at all, and he didn't like having to hurt her.

Andrew reached for the cup of coffee Bill set in front of him. Cora had given up and gone back to her parents', not quite sure where she was heading, but knowing she had to do something.

"What did you find, Andrew?" Bill's voice was quiet. "You're not here just to visit."

Andrew gave a small tired smile. It had been a long day. He was missing Bill on the investigative team. "Sure, I am. But you're right. There is something strange about Cora's husband." He sipped his coffee, gathering his thoughts. "He just doesn't exist. And now that you tell me all the documentation she had on him is gone that makes it even more strange."

Bill nodded. "It does. I have a feeling this is just beginning for her. Her place being tossed the way it was? They were looking for something, and I think it was her photos. She really doesn't have a lot of Nigel, or whoever he is."

"I did some research on that West character and I have Lily working on it as well." He paused, gathering his thoughts. "What all has Cora said about him? What are your impressions? You know her. I don't."

Bill paused, thinking through what the two had discussed that day and what he had found out. "I think whoever searched her apartment was looking for more than just the photos or Weston's identification. He seems to have been involved in something really dark. Given he said he was a botanist, I'm thinking drugs. The thing is, I checked with the university he was to have graduated from. There is no record of him. I can't even find a photo of him in any of their year books."

Andrew nodded. "That's about what I thought you'd find. Even the name you gave me doesn't fit him. Lily's working on trying to track down more information on him but we really don't have much to work with."

Bill sighed, his thumb rubbing around the rim of his mug, his eyes focused on the verse printed on it. He had read it so many times but the reminder that he was to lift his eyes to the hills, where he got his strength and help, always calmed him. "Now what, Andrew? If it was a regular case, we'd have to let it go."

"I know we would, but I don't want to. She's too important to you, Bill."

Bill shot Andrew a startled look.

"She's a good friend of yours, Bill. You have a history there that we can't ignore." Andrew studied him. "What are the chances someone is after you and using Cora?"

Bill stilled. "What do you mean?"

"Just what I said. Why would Elizabeth's information and photo be in Cora's apartment unless Weston was somehow involved in her death?"

Bill sat back in his chair, chills running through him. "Drugs. A new drug that can't be traced or leaves little to no evidence after a certain length of time." He shook his head, biting his lip to control his emotions. "Maybe that's why we couldn't explain Elizabeth's death. There was no evidence." He was on his feet, heading to his office. "I'll be right back."

He sat once more, opening the folder he had placed on the table, searching for the coroner's report. He tapped it. "Right here. I always wondered about that. There was a bruise on her inner arm with a small speck of blood. No one could explain what or why." He looked up at Andrew. "If she was given an injection that killed her, and there was no evidence to suggest a drug overdose, then we wouldn't have looked for it."

Andrew nodded, compassion in his gaze. "That's exactly what I think happened. I talked to the medical examiner here and showed him the report. That's what he picked up on right away."

Bill sighed. "We can't prove anything now, not that way." He could feel the anger growing within him. "I want whoever it was Weston was working with. And I want him to pay for any deaths he's caused."

"It could be a woman too, you know." Andrew reached for his phone as he felt it vibrate. "It's Emma." He listened as Emma spoke rapidly, taking notes before he slid his phone away and sat for a moment before he looked up at Bill.

Bill waited expectantly, knowing Andrew would speak when he was ready.

"Emma's done a good piece of work, Bill. She's managed to track Nigel Weston's documents. They were fake, as we supposed, and she's had Abe talk to the man who forged them. Abe took Micah with him."

Bill grinned for a moment. "Micah knows how to intimidate well, especially if it's computer related." He sobered. "What else?"

"The forger has agreed to speak with us. I'll send Lily over tomorrow to do just that." Andrew sighed. "I don't know how much further we'll get though. I pray that we get somewhere."

Bill stood, heading for the coffee pot. He held it up at Andrew, who shook his head. "Cora's really hurting, Andrew. She's having to come to terms with knowing that the man she loved and married wasn't who he said he was."

Andrew nodded. "I know. It's not easy for her. Has she said much at all?"

Bill shook his head. "She was really upset when she found his identification missing, then to hear what I found." He stared out the kitchen window, his back to Andrew for a moment before he turned. "I still don't get why that would be there. As far as I know, Elizabeth didn't know this man."

"But she may well have known someone connected to him. What you said happened before she died is all likely related in some manner. We just have to figure it out." Andrew shoved back from the table and stood, reaching for his mug and carrying it to the sink, where he rinsed it out. "I'm off now, Bill. Call me if Cora remembers anything else. And don't forget. You are on vacation. Find some time to do some fun stuff."

Bill laughed as he followed Andrew to the door. "I intend to. Wesley and I are planning on hiking overnight this week. We haven't had a chance to do that in about a year."

"Say hi to him for me. He's become a stranger, you know."

Bill nodded. "He has. His work has him immersed too much." Bill stopped speaking, his eyes flying to Andrew. "Now, why didn't I think of that? Wesley could help research what's been going on. He's on that task force about those new designer drugs. He's sorry he's not out on the streets making arrests, but maybe, just maybe, he might have some insight." Bill's brother had been a street cop, recruited to serve on a county and city drug task force.

Andrew nodded. "Talk to him when you're hiking. See what he has to say."

Bill watched Andrew walk to his car before he turned, locking the door behind him. He stretched. It had been a long stressful emotional day and he was exhausted, but he knew he would never sleep. He headed for his office, but instead of working, he reached for his Bible. He desperately needed some God time. He could feel the onslaught coming and he wanted to be prepared.

His thoughts slipped to Cora and he smiled. She was such a special person, he thought. Then he frowned. How could anyone take advantage of her like Weston had? His thoughts moved to the photos she had downloaded for him. A sudden idea had him pulling up the folder they were in and he studied each one, conviction growing that he knew what it was all about. But how could he prove it?

Chapter 6

Cora looked askance at Bill as he stood in her parents' kitchen, not quite sure she had heard him right.

"Are you really saying you think Elizabeth died from a drug overdose? How can that be? I doubt she'd be using drugs, knowing how you feel about them."

"That's just a supposition we're making. It would explain a finding in the original coroner's report that was overlooked."

Cora's eyes flew to the ceiling as she wrapped her arms around herself and began pacing. "Where does it end, Bill? What all was Nigel involved in?"

Bill leaned against the counter, his hands gripping the edge, his eyes on Cora's father standing back in the hallway where she couldn't see him. He saw the sorrow on Mr. Brodie's face and sighed. There was nothing he could do to alleviate her pain, and he only seemed to be making it worse.

57

"I don't know, Cora. We're working on it. I'm going to talk with Wesley when we go hiking later this week and see what he's been hearing about new drugs."

She spun to stare at him. "Wesley? Why him? What would he know about drugs?"

Bill stared at her, not quite sure how to handle the anger bristling from her. He opened his mouth, but before he could speak, her father spoke from behind her.

"Lose the attitude, Coretta!" She spun, staring at him. "Bill's grieving too. His brother is on a drug task force and likely knows more than any of us what drugs are new and dangerous."

Cora shot her father a look of anger, then brushed by him to head for the back yard. He sighed as he stared after her before turning to Bill.

"I'm sorry, Bill, about your loss. We had no idea until Cora said something the other day."

Bill shrugged. "It wasn't something I felt I could share with people here in town. We hadn't been back in so long, I don't think people really knew Elizabeth and I were that serious." He nodded towards where Cora had gone. "She needs to be very careful. Someone is after her and won't stop, not until she's hurt or dead."

Her father nodded, a sober look on his face. "I hear you, Bill. But I'm not sure Cora really understands that."

"Not likely. She likely won't unless something happens. I need you and Mrs. Brodie to be very careful as well. They may go after you to hurt her."

Cora's father nodded. "We realize that and are taking precautions as well."

Bill shook the hand extended to him and then excused himself. He needed some time to think and being there wasn't allowing that. He headed for his favourite section of the river bank and walked along it until he found the fallen tree he had come to think of as his.

Lost in thought, he didn't hear the running footsteps until he felt himself locked in arms and tumbled to the ground. He fought to get away, but the two men holding him prevailed, and he was shoved face first down into the sand. He struggled to rise, stopping as he felt the round metal object tucked into his neck at the base of his skull. He froze, not sure who had attacked him or why. He was dragged to his feet and a blindfold tied tight over his eyes.

Forced to walk forward, he stumbled over the rough ground, only staying upright by the tight grip he was held in. Finally, he was shoved into a building, at least he thought it was, falling to his hands and knees with the force of the push. He heard the door lock behind him, and after waiting, he reached to pull the blindfold off his eyes. He squinted, trying to focus in the dimness.

He rose to his feet, his eyes roaming the small building. He knew it. It had been standing empty for years after having been used as a hunt cabin, until it was abandoned and fell into disarray. It wouldn't hold him long, he knew. He felt for the corner he had discovered one day not long before that had really weakened and pried at the boards, the wood falling to bits under his fingers.

He shot a quick glance over his shoulder towards the door, not certain how much time he would have. He dug quicker at the rotten wood, his fingers flying. He finally managed to dig out enough wood he could pry at a board and then a second one, giving just enough room for him to slide out and run for the trees behind the cabin. He ran towards the river, knowing he could follow it back. And if he remembered, one of his friends always hid a canoe there. He turned as he heard shouts behind him and then picked up his speed. He slid to a stop at the river bank and looking around, spied the canoe. Quickly he launched it, jumping in and paddling away as he heard running footsteps behind him. He pulled up under an overhanging branch.

He listened to the men who were searching for him, hearing the curses and the blame being given. His head went down as he recognized two of the voices. They were not who he ever thought would be involved in something like this.

He finally paddled away, his craft silent on the water, as he headed for the river bank where he had parked his car. He drew up the canoe, tying it off and then pulling out his phone to call his friend. Getting only voice mail, he left a quick message and then headed for home. He had research to do and then he'd need to speak with Andrew. He sighed. Andrew would not be happy to hear from him, he knew that already.

Cora paced, her parents watching her closely before exchanging glances.

"Cora." When she ignored her father, he spoke again, his voice hard and angry. "Cora! Sit!"

She glared at him before she slammed herself into a chair.

"Enough of the attitude, young lady. There are other people concerned in this situation besides yourself. Your mother and I have to take precautions too." Her father stared at her until she lowered her eyes.

"Andrew has been around. He's talked to your mother and I. Bill went missing earlier today. They found his car but not him. That was after he was here."

Cora's glance flew to her father and then to her mother. "Bill? Why? How?"

"Andrew doesn't know." Robinson Brodie shared a look with his wife, Maggie. "They're looking for him right now, but don't have much to work with. You may know where he would have gone."

She shook her head. "It's been too many years, Dad. I don't know where he'd go. Not any more." Sadness crept through her that she had lost touch with someone who had been such a good friend.

Rob Brodie picked up his phone as it rang and listened, his eyes sliding shut with relief. He set it down, his eyes on his wife, who nodded.

"Bill's safe, Cora. Andrew didn't have many details yet but he was on his way to see him."

Cora shoved back her chair to stand but her father's hand on her arm stopped her. "You can't go to him, Cora. Not this way. You need to decide what he is to you, a friend, an acquaintance, or something more."

Cora stared at her father, then at her mother, seeing her nod in agreement. She sighed. "I don't know how I feel, Dad. Everything has been so tossed up in the air with everything I've learned about Nigel and then about Bill." She looked down, swallowing hard. "I promise I'll do my best not to hurt him."

"Your best might not be enough, Cora." Her mother's voice was soft. "You have never come to terms with Nigel's death. You've hidden everything deep inside. It's time you did deal with it. It now involves more than just you, or just us." She shared another look with Rob. "We never told you, hoping we had heard wrong, but Nigel told us a week before the wedding that we wouldn't see you much, maybe once or twice a year.

You would be his and his only from the date of the wedding and moving forward."

Cora stared at her mother, horrified. "I would never have let that happen."

"It would have, Cora. It would have." Maggie brushed back tears. "We didn't know how to tell you. We should have. Maybe if we had, you wouldn't have gone through what you went through."

Cora stood, sorrow on her face, a heart heavy with grief. Her parents watched, then her father spoke.

"Go talk with Silas, Cora. He'll help you."

She nodded. "Maybe, but with him married to Madigan, it makes it difficult."

"It shouldn't. He won't say a word about what you two talked about, not even to Madigan, not unless you tell him it's okay."

"I've never talked to a minister who has been able to keep a secret yet. Somehow, I don't trust that he will."

"Cora, please talk to Silas. He's been through a lot and knows how dangerous life can be."

She finally nodded. "I'll think about it. No promises. Now, what about Bill?"

Chapter 7

$\mathcal{B}$ill looked up as Andrew stopped in his office doorway, shooting a glance towards him and then back towards the rest of the department. He finally entered, closing the door, and sank into his chair behind his desk, fatigue weighing him down, a sigh escaping him, his eyes on Bill.

Finally, he spoke. "Okay, Bill. What happened to you?"

Bill shrugged. "I was just sitting there by the river when I was attacked by two men, blindfolded and then walked to the old Harris hunt cabin. It's in such bad shape I was able to get out and get away." He paused, a shadow on his face. "I heard them talking. I know two of them." He named names and Andrew paled.

"You're absolutely sure?"

Bill nodded. "Without a shadow of a doubt. Now, how do I face Wesley knowing task force members attacked me?"

Andrew shook his head. "You need to talk to him and today. He needs to know." He looked up and then rose to answer the knock at his door, surprised to see the man standing there.

"Wesley. We were just talking about you."

"Have you seen Bill? You called looking for him. I can't find him and someone said he had gone missing."

Andrew stepped back so Wesley could enter. Bill had risen as he heard his brother's voice.

Wesley stood for a moment, then reached to hug his brother, holding tight for a few minutes before he stepped back.

"Are you okay?" Bill could hear the concern in his brother's voice.

"I am. What are you doing here?"

"I should be asking you that." Wesley stared at his brother.

"What do you mean?"

"Can we sit? I think this will take a while." Wesley stared at Bill even as he sat. "Bill, what's going on?"

"What do you mean, what's going on?" Bill stared at his brother, almost like looking into a mirror except Wesley's hair was longer and he had a neatly trimmed beard.

"That's what I want to know. I had a feeling something was up with you. I came looking for you. You didn't answer your phone. You're not at your home. I get a call from Andrew asking if I had seen you, that they had found your car by the river but not you." Wesley's concerned eyes searched his brother's face. "So what happened?"

Bill quickly brought his brother up to the present on what all had happened in the last few days.

"Cora Brodie? You've been in contact with her?" When Bill nodded, Wesley's head went back as he stared at the ceiling before looking over at Andrew. "That complicates things."

"What do you mean, complicates things? I'm not going to avoid an old friend."

Wesley held up a hand at his brother's words. "I know you won't and I don't expect you to." He reached for the folder he had dropped on Andrew's desk. "Here. Read this. There's two copies, Andrew." He had each man a stack of papers. When Bill went to question him, he shook his head. "Read. Then we talk."

Bill reached for a pen from the holder on Andrew's desk before he had finished the first page, making notes and underlining as he went along. He reached for a highlighting marker as well. Wesley's eyes closed as he prayed, knowing that what he had just shared with his brother would devastate him and bring out the anger in him. That was not what his intent had been. He had needed to do this. The task force was making headway but there was still a lot of work that needed to be done. He had been told he needed to talk to his brother by the task force head. He hadn't been given a choice, he knew.

Bill finally sat back, thoughtful before he turned to Andrew. "Is this what you've been thinking, Andrew?" At his nod, he turned to his brother. "How'd you get all this information, Wes?"

"Informants. Lots of digging. Old reports." He shared a look with Andrew. "I hated to bring Elizabeth into this, Bill."

Bill nodded, a look of sorrow flashing across his face, so quickly the other two men weren't sure they had even seen it. "It's okay. But how did you tie Cora's husband into this?"

"It wasn't hard. He's been on the radar for years. We finally tracked down his name. Darius Lock."

Bill's eyes shot up at that. "Lock? Wasn't he here for your first year in high school and then moved?"

Wesley nodded. "He was. He kept to himself. No one seems to have known him too well but he seems to have known all of us too well. I think he was stalking Cora all along, and the leader of the cartel he became involved in knew this and used it to his advantage. Cora wouldn't have known him. I checked. There doesn't seem to have been any path that they crossed."

Bill stared down at his notes. "Andrew, I want off vacation."

"Not happening, Bill. I need you to stick as close to Cora as she will allow. From what I can gather, they'll be after her. They've already proven that. In fact, I think they'll be after both of you."

Bill finally agreed, not happy with Andrew's directive, but knowing he would follow through. He didn't want anything to happen to his friend. "Wes, what did you mean in this where you think I was the target?"

"I was waiting for you to pick up on that. How well did you know him?"

Bill shrugged. "I'd see him around school, around town. I didn't know him at all. Didn't know any of his friends. Why?"

"We served a search warrant on his parents' place. His mother still had some of his possessions. We're working through them but you are named in papers we've found. There is evidence that he stalked Elizabeth. He knew you two were married and had decided to use her for an experiment of a new drug, somehow to get back at you for something we have no idea what." Sorrow crossed his face as he watched Bill try to comprehend that. "I'm sorry, Bill. There is no easy way to continue. We know he was involved in finding plants that could be used in new designer drugs. Plants we wouldn't have thought to be used in that way.

"We think that's why he started tracking Cora and finally made contact with her. She's known for her travelogues of her tours to find unusual items - plants included. From what we can determine, it wasn't to have gone as far as it did. He was going to use her and then throw her away."

Bill's eyes were glued to his brother's and he heard Andrew say something, not catching what he said.

"That's right, Andrew. He had no intention of marrying her. He wanted to be part of what she was finding, but not at the cost of his freedom. We have evidence that he planned to walk away from her that day, but something happened. We have no idea what but the speculation was that he was told he couldn't or she would suffer the consequences. There is no evidence that he really cared for her or loved her. The opposite, in fact. As to why he stepped in front of her, we don't know the reasoning but video the photographer took shows Cora moving around him and that put him into the path of the knife. She essentially saved her own life."

"She's struggling with knowing she was used. I have no idea how she'll take this news, Wes. Maybe you need to be with me when I talk to her." He pulled out his phone as it vibrated in his pocket. "It's Cora. She's asking if I can meet her in about an hour."

"Why don't the two of you go meet her?" Andrew stood. "Let me work through what you've asked, Wesley, and then I'll call you."

Bill stood, his eyes on Andrew, before he nodded and motioned to Wesley. He followed his brother from the department building, then stopped.

"I don't have my car. Andrew said they had it taken to my place."

Wesley pointed to his truck. "We can use mine. Let's go find your lady, Bill."

Bill shot him a look but didn't correct him. He had often thought of Cora as just that, his lady, during high school but college and Elizabeth had changed that thinking. It seemed as if his thinking was heading back that way.

He shut the truck door at the park and hesitated, saying a prayer for guidance and wisdom and another for his friend. What he and Wesley would have to tell her would be difficult for her to hear. He would have given just about anything not to be the one who had to tell her, but he wasn't given much choice.

Cora looked as Bill and Wesley sat on either side of her. She had chosen a sheltered bench, under a spreading oak tree just out in leaf.

"Wesley! I didn't expect to see you." She reached to hug him, then sat back, her head turning as she studied first one man and then the other. "Bill?"

Bill stared into the distance, not quite sure how to proceed. He felt Cora's hand on his arm and reached to cover hers.

"Wesley has some information he needs to share with you. Before he does, we need to pray. What he will share won't be pretty, Cora." His eyes on her face, he still hesitated to continue to speak.

Cora eyed him, then held up her rings. "Any worse than this? The diamond? Cubic zirconia. The gold band? Gold plated. There's writing on the inside of the bands that the jeweller didn't understand."

Wesley reached for them, squinting as he studied the writing. "You said you had a break-in?" At her nod, he motioned to the rings. "This is what they were after. Bill, you need to get them to Andrew. Today."

"I will, but first we need to talk, Cora." He drew a deep breath and then proceeded to tell her what all they had found out, including Nigel's correct name.

"Darius Lock? That was him? I always thought Nigel reminded me of someone but I never dreamed it was him."

"How did you know him?" Bill watched her carefully.

She shook her head. "I didn't. That's the thing. I didn't like the group he hung around with. I just vaguely remember seeing him a few times with that group."

Wesley and Bill exchanged glances over her head. "What was it about the group you didn't like?" Bill's voice was quiet.

She shrugged. "I don't know. I think they're the ones who were doing the break-ins that year in the ritzy neighbourhood of Oak City. Rumours went around. I think they were also into drugs."

"That would fit with what we've been able to dig up on him, Cora." Wesley ran his hand through his hair, lost in thought.

Bill suddenly rose, catching Cora's hand in his, and walking rapidly towards Wesley's truck, Wesley keeping pace with him.

Cora struggled to get her hand loose from Bill's but his grip tightened even firmer. "Bill. Let me go!"

"Into the truck, Cora. Now!" Bill almost shoved her into the back seat and then slammed the door, crawling into the front seat as Wesley started his vehicle and pulled away.

"Bill? What was that all about?" Cora was angry.

"You didn't see them?" He spun in his seat, his eyes hard, as he questioned her. "There were three men headed our way. I know one of them. He's a known criminal and always up to be a gun for hire. They weren't walking our way for their health."

Cora paled even as she looked at Wesley for confirmation. He nodded, compassion in his glance. "I didn't see them, Bill. Really, I didn't." She slumped back in the seat. "Why are they after me?"

Bill stared at her for a moment before his expression softened. Wesley nodded to himself. Bill has gone past Elizabeth, he thought. He shot a glance into the rearview mirror and caught the look on Cora's face. And she's not grieving for old what's-his-name any more. Thank you, Lord.

"Like we said, Lock was using you to find new sources of plants for their drugs. Whoever employed him thinks you have evidence against them." He tapped his shirt pocket where he had placed her rings. "And these are the clue. I'll pass them on to our lab and see what they can come up with." He paused, a sudden horrible thought crossing his mind. "Did you find yourself followed a lot over the last year?"

She nodded, not quite sure why he was asking that particular question.

"I suspect there's a computer chip in one of your rings that tracks your movements. That's how they knew you weren't home and could search your place."

She paled, the thought that she had been tracked not sitting well with her. "He did that?"

Bill turned to Wesley as he parked in front of the police department. "I'll only be a couple of minutes. Let me take Cora in with me. That way, if Andrew has any questions, she's inside."

Wesley nodded. "I'll be here." He watched as Bill hurried Cora into the building before he stood, leaning on his truck, eyes searching the area. He could feel someone out there, just not see them.

Andrew looked up as Bill and Cora appeared in his doorway, then sat back, his pen still in his hand. "What are you doing back here, Bill? And with Cora?"

Bill pulled out Cora's rings from the pocket he had stuck them in. "These.

There's writing on them. Wesley and I think this is what they were after in the break-ins."

Andrew reached for them, studied them and then slid them into an evidence bag. "I'll get them to the lab. Right now, though, I think we need to put you two somewhere safe."

Cora stood, her eyes flashing. "I'm not running and hiding, not a chance of that." She was out of the office and disappeared before either man could stop her.

Bill stood, staring after her. "Did she really just do that?"

Andrew started to laugh. "She did, my friend. That she did. You have a handful there, you know?"

Bill's head whipped around at the words and then he shook it. "Not a chance, Andrew. Not a chance."

Sudden commotion from the front of the building had Andrew sliding by Bill and heading that way, finding all the officers there crouching under cover. Bill gave an exclamation and tried to brush past Andrew only to find himself slammed back by Andrew's arm against the wall in the hall.

"Wesley's out there, Andrew. I need to get to him."

Andrew nodded. "I know he is. We have officers out there. They have protection. You don't."

Bill tried to head around him, to find himself slammed harder into the wall, Andrew's hand holding him in place even as Andrew ducked his head to see out the window.

"Andrew!"

"I know, Bill. But you can't go out there. For one thing, you don't have your weapon. Now, back off and let the others do their job."

Bill's head rested back on the wall and his eyes slid shut in prayer, frustration and worry on his face and in his attitude. He didn't think they had ever been under attack this way at the department. His head popped up as his eyes flew open.

"Where's Cora?" He searched the area around them, frantic to find her.

Andrew turned, catching sight of another detective, Lily, standing in the hallway, pointing at the break room.

"Lily has her. She's safe." His attention went back to the front. "Pete?"

"One shooter, Chief. On the building across the way. ETF's working their way around there. Sam's out front with whoever it was that was in the truck."

"Bill's brother and a fellow officer from Oak City. Any word if they're hurt?"

"Haven't heard, and I can't see. Every time one of us looks up, he starts shooting again." The speaker ducked down again as another rain of bullets sprinkled across the front of the building. "Much more of this and that glass is going to give way."

Andrew nodded, then turning, shoved Bill towards Lily. "I think he's seeing you in here, Bill. Get back with Cora and Lily. Maybe then we'll have a chance to stop him." He answered his phone, his eyes darting after Bill as he heard Sam's voice and his report, his heart hurting already for Bill.

Bill nodded even as he ducked and ran towards the break room. Cora looked up as he ran into it, then was across the room, the force of her body hitting him slamming him against the closed door. His arms wrapped around her even as her own arms hugged him tight.

"Bill! I thought you were hurt." Cora's voice was choked with tears.

Bill shared a look with Lily, who nodded her head. Cora had tried to get out of the room then, he knew.

"I'm fine, Cora. Let's get you sitting down." He gave a low laugh as she refused to release him, refused to move. "Come on, darlin'. Let's get us sitting down, okay?"

She finally nodded, but still didn't move. Bill shook his head, finally reaching to sweep her into his arms and then walking over to sit on the couch near the inside wall. He sank down, cradling her on his knee, her face hidden against him.

Lily sat beside them, her hand reaching out to lightly rub Cora's back. "He's fine, Cora. Just like I promised." She shared a look with Bill, a question in her glance.

He shook his head, not wanting to say much in front of Cora. "We have a shooter. The ETF team's out there."

"I hope no one has been hurt."

Bill's face shadowed. "So do I. My brother was out front when this started." He looked up as the door opened and Andrew slipped in, his heart falling at the look on Andrew's face.

"How's Cora?" Andrew gave a small grin at Bill's discomfort.

"If I could see her face, I might be able to tell you. She just won't look up." He stared down at the dark head of hair tight to him. "It's okay, Cora. If Andrew's in here, it's over. Come on, darlin'. Are you going to look up at me?" He gave a low laugh as she shook her head. "Okay, then. We'll sit here for a bit." He looked up at Andrew.

"Wesley's been hit, Bill. Not serious. More like a graze on his upper arm. He saw movement and was going down when he was hit. He's refusing to seek treatment, not until he knows you two are safe."

"Us?"

Andrew nodded. "ETF caught the guy. He was hired over the phone to take you and Cora out. He has no idea who hired him or why."

Bill slowly nodded, his eyes first on Andrew, then dropping to Cora. "What have we gotten mixed up in, Andrew? I don't like being on this side of the game."

Andrew and Lily both laughed at the expression on his face as well as his words.

"I didn't either, Bill, but you know Phoebe and I came through it." Andrew leaned back against the wall, his eyes thoughtful, hands jammed into his pockets.

"I'll send on the rings to the lab and put a rush on it. This whole thing just now changes it all. At some point, we may need to look at sticking you two away somewhere."

Bill nodded, not happy with the prospect. "Just don't talk to Silas, okay?"

Andrew started to laugh even harder. "Why? Don't want to take the route Phoebe and I did or that Silas and Madigan took?" Both couples had married very quickly, thinking the only way to keep the ladies safe was marriage.

"No!" Bill was adamant in that. "If and when I marry again, I want to court the lady in proper style before we wed, not after the fact." He sighed, missing the surprised look on Lily's face. Andrew saw it and knew she'd have questions for him later. "That didn't come out right. I'm sorry. I know you and Silas and all our friends still court your wives."

Lily started laughing at the look on Bill's face. "It can happen both ways, Bill. Make it a lifelong courtship. That's what my parents have done."

He nodded, his eyes on Cora's face as she finally lifted her head, devastation on her face.

He looked past Andrew as the door opened and Wesley appeared, his jacket in his hands, his left sleeve ripped away and a bandage on the upper arm.

"Wesley?"

"I'm okay, Bill. Just a nick." Wesley shook his head at his brother as his eyes sought Cora's face. "I'm just glad no one else was hurt. Now, how be we get you two out of here? Andrew sending a couple of patrol officers with us."

Chapter 8

Slamming the door to the shed at the back of her parents' property open in anger, Cora stood, looking around, waving at the dust flying in front of her face. She had had enough of someone running her life. It was time she took hers back. She glanced behind her. She had managed to make her getaway from the house before Bill showed up, and show up she knew he would. He hadn't been letting her out of his sight, and she wasn't quite sure how she felt about that.

At one time, during their last year of high school, she thought their feelings for one another were gathering strength. Then they were their separate ways to college and he just cut off contact with her. She had been hurt and angry at him. She knew now that he had found a lady to love who had loved him back as he should have been. She also knew that she hadn't been the one at the time and didn't even know now how she felt about him.

She stared around, not quite sure why she had come out there, but something had compelled her to come. She walked through to the shelving at the back, searching through the boxes until she found the one she wanted, dragging it down to the floor. Her hands resting on the top of it, she hesitated, before conviction swept over her. Her attitude was wrong, and she knew it. Her head bowed as she prayed for forgiveness and strength and wisdom to get through what she feared was coming.

She pulled the flaps open, even as she sat on the floor, reaching into the box and pulling out mementos from high school. She smiled sadly at some, brushed away a few tears, before she reached for the last item. She pulled it out, setting it aside and dumping everything back into the box, before she rose to set the box back on the shelf. She dropped to the floor once more, her hand on the decorated metal box.

Her finger slowed its rubbing on the box as she heard footsteps and saw sneakers stop in front of her. She sighed inwardly. Bill had arrived.

"Go away, Bill."

A soft laugh caused her to raise her head. "Sorry, Cora. I'm not Bill." Andrew stood in front of her, his eyes thoughtful, a smile on his face, dressed casually in jeans, a sweatshirt and sneakers.

"Chief McBeth? To what do I owe the honour?" She glanced at him and then looked back down at the box. "You're not dressed up today."

Andrew dropped to a sitting position in front of her, a smile on his face at her avoidance of him. "It's Andrew, please. I'd like to think we could be friends. I know Phoebe wants to get to know you. And I took a personal day today. Phoebe wanted me to do something with her."

She shrugged. "Whatever." She glanced back at him, not able to read him. "Did you track me down for a reason or just for that?"

"I'm serious when I said Phoebe wants to be your friend. If you're going to be around, I know Bill wants to stay in touch with you. That means we'll be in touch. I'd like to think of you as a friend."

She shrugged once more. "I have no idea where I'll be, but I'm not sure it will be in this town." She sighed as she lifted the lid from the box. "I came out here, looking for something, I have no idea what." She carefully lifted medals and papers and photos from the box, her hand stilling as she reached the bottom. "Now, what is this? It's not mine."

Andrew moved closer, his hand going out to stop hers. "Let me see, please, Cora." He studied the object on the bottom of the box. "It looks like a thumb drive. You wouldn't have had it during high school. Not this design." He looked up at her. "Any reason to suspect Lock came out here and hid this?"

She looked up at him, startled. "It's possible. He rarely came home with me but he did about a month before he died. He disappeared for about 20 minutes. I thought he was just walking around the yard. He must have done this." Anger began to build once more in her. "What all did he do, Andrew? How much more am I to suffer because of him?"

Andrew studied her face and then looked down into the box. "Do you have a bag or envelope I can use?"

She nodded, rising to find one from the shelving. "Mom stores extra stuff out here, if she's found a bargain." She handed him a bag before sinking back to the floor and gathering up the memories she had dumped on the floor. "Do you need the box?"

He shook his head. "No, this is fine." He watched her for a moment. "I can't say enough how sorry I am for what you're going through." He held up a hand as she went to speak. "Just let me say a couple of things, okay? Then we can talk. Our team's been tracking Lock. He's been watching you for years, long before he made contact with you. We have no idea why that would be. We know he made contact with you once you started posting about the plants you were finding. Secondly, Bill is very worried about his friend, and that worry has carried through to all his friends. We don't want you hurt or worse." He studied her face again. "We need to think of a way to keep you safe. Bill's in danger too, just why we're working on."

"Where is he, anyway? I thought he'd be out here by now." Cora leaned to the side to look around Andrew.

Andrew started laughing, causing her eyes to fly to his. "Bill's not coming today or tomorrow, Cora. He and Wesley are on one of their overnight hiking trips."

"Bill? Hiking? That's not him."

"It is. I've known him since he joined the county force and he and Wesley have been hiking since before then. He told me last night that Elizabeth liked to hike and she started him on that. At first, he kept it up to keep connected to her memory. Now, he and Wesley do it in order to spend time with one another. Now, is there anything else you've remembered or thought of?"

She shook her head and stood, the box in her hand. "I don't think so. If I do I'll call you." She pointed at the bag in his hand. "I don't want to know what's on that."

"We may have to talk about it, Cora, at some point." Andrew watched as she finally nodded. "It may be nothing, but somehow I don't think that's the case. If it's not yours, then it must be Lock's."

"I don't know, Andrew." She looked at the bag, then back up at him. "I'm not sure whose it is. It could be anyone's."

"I doubt that. Someone had to know that box was important to you to have hidden this away in it." Andrew finally walked away, his thoughts on Cora.

Cora stared after Andrew for a moment before she too rose and left the shed, carefully closing the door and locking it after herself. She headed for the house. She was restless and realized she had come to depend on Bill being around, even though it had only been a few days. She needed to get over that.

She found her mother in the kitchen, stopped for a few words, and then headed for her bedroom. She grabbed her jacket and hat and the camera she loved the best and headed out, walking through her town, stopping every once in a while to shoot a photo or a bit of video. She had an assignment due in about a week and hadn't had any idea of what she wanted to do. Now she did. She shot a quick text off to her editor and then continued on her tour of the town, ending up near the river. She stopped, her eyes seeing the changes time had wrought in her town.

Bill stood on the hill overlooking Oak City and waited for Wesley to catch up with him. He lifted his face to the setting sun and felt its warmth filter through him as he closed his eyes. He had needed this time away. Thank you, Lord, that this was already planned because I don't think I'd have left town otherwise. Protect Cora, please. I don't want my friend hurt. Cover her in the hollow of Your hand.

He turned as he heard footsteps stop beside him and Wesley stood there, matching him in height and build, both lean and tall, his eyes searching Bill's face.

"Thinking about Cora?"

"How'd you know?" Bill shot a quick look at his brother before he turned to walk towards the upward trail.

"She's always been able to get under your skin, whether you realized it or not. Leave her with God, Willow. Leave her with God."

Bill stopped, gathering his emotions before he turned to face his brother, blinking back tears at a nickname not used in many years. "You haven't called me that since Mom and Dad died."

Wesley nodded. "I know. You're so like the willow Dad nicknamed you after - bending with the wind but always snapping back. You needed that reminder today, Bill."

Bill stared at his brother, unable to speak for a moment. His brother knew him so well. "So, how much do you think Lock was involved in the drug trade here?"

"Deeply, very deeply. Had been since he was a teenager. Cora was right when she said he was involved when he lived here. We've talked to old friends of his and they confirmed it." He sighed. "There's still a lot of work to do but I have a feeling there are people on the task force who shouldn't be and are hindering our work."

"There are, at least two. You need to talk to Andrew."

"I will. He did give me a couple of names. He said you passed them on to him." He stopped walking, reaching out to stop Bill. "What's your take on this, Bill?"

Bill shrugged. "I have no idea. I have no idea why we were tossed over the railing the first day I saw her after all those years. Faith said she thought she knew the men but she couldn't be sure. More of an impression she got." He turned to look around him, taking in the early spring foliage. "I think it comes back to Lock. Something that happened years ago. Something he thought Cora or I saw and that we didn't or that we thought was so insignificant that we don't remember it. Something that he said to someone or showed someone and they've connected it to us. I just don't know, Wesley."

"I think you may be right, Bill." He nodded ahead of them. "There's the cabin. I don't think it's changed in all these years."

Bill stopped, his eyes on the cabin, memories flooding through him. Memories of hiking here with Elizabeth, with Wesley and Anna, then with just Wesley. He blinked at the strong emotion he felt, waiting for the pain to hit that always hit when he thought of Elizabeth but it didn't hit that day. He paused, his thoughts on his wife, then on Cora. Lord, are You telling me it's time to move on? To find another lady to love, to share my life with?

Wesley clasped his brother's shoulder for a moment before he moved past and into the cabin. His heart broke for his brother but felt hope that just maybe Bill had started healing. Bless Cora, he thought, if she's the one God is using.

Chapter 9

*C*ora stood just inside the church door that Sunday morning, unsure if she really wanted to be there. She hadn't waited for her parents, walking from their home before they even knew she had left the house. She looked behind her, wondering if she had enough courage to turn and walk back out. A touch on her arm had her jumping in fright and then spinning to see who had touched her. She frowned, trying to remember who of their friends it was. Jonah. That's who.

"Cora? Are you okay? Sorry. I didn't mean to frighten you." Jonah's brow furrowed, his eyes searching her face before he lifted them to seek the platform where Bill was practicing with the worship team.

"I'm fine, Jonah. Just not sure if I should be here."

"You should. Do you have a seat you were wanting to sit in today?"

She shook her head. "Not really. I don't want to sit with Mom and Dad. I never liked sitting that close to the front."

Jonah laughed. "Neither did I. Couldn't make a quick getaway that close to the pastor, now could we?" He pointed to a pew near the back. "Why don't you sit with Candace and me? Bill will be down to join us once the worship team is done."

"Bill? In the worship team?" Cora was surprised. She shivered as she turned to look around her, feeling eyes on her but not seeing anyone watching her.

"You feel the eyes?" Jonah smiled in sympathy as she shot him a quick look. "We felt them, too, Candace and I. Always felt them watching us."

Cora groaned. "Not another one of you!"

Jonah started to laugh. "Yep. Now, do you want to sit beside Candace or on the end?"

"On the end, I think."

"And no making a fast getaway before Bill gets down here." Jonah smirked at her look of outrage even as Candace started to laugh at his nonsense.

Bill hesitated a moment before sliding into the seat beside Cora. He really hadn't expected her to be in church today, or to have saved a seat for him. He exchanged a glance with Jonah, who nodded at Cora. Bill got the message. Something was up and he would find out after the service.

Bill waited for Cora to stand at the end of the service, his eyes on her face, a frown on his. She wasn't moving, her eyes focused on the front before she turned to him, a fierce look in her eyes.

"Why would God care that much, Bill? Why would He ever care what happens to us? Why would He hide us in the hollow of His hand, if I understand Silas right?"

Bill slid back down into the pew, his eyes on her even as he reached for her hand, clasping her cold fingers in his. "Because He loves us that much, Cora, enough to protect us."

She snorted. "I don't think so, Bill. God doesn't care that much. If He had, why did I go through what I did? Why did Elizabeth die?"

Bill sighed, knowing it would be a long conversation and not an easy one. "Because that's who He is. Listen, I can see if Silas can explain it better than I can."

She shook her head. "No, thanks. Any pastor I've ever talked to has turned right around and told what I said. So why would I trust him?”

Bill’s eyes caught Silas’ as Silas hesitated behind Cora, not wanting to interrupt.

“Cora, Silas is here. I can guarantee you he won’t say one word of what you ask or tell him, not unless you give permission. He won’t even tell Madigan you’ve talked, if that’s what you want.”

She turned to study him, then shook her head. “I’m sorry.” She was up and on her feet, brushing past Bill to head from the church.

Silas turned. “Go after her, Bill. She’s not safe. Bring her tonight to the dinner, if she’ll come.”

“I can’t guarantee she will. At one time, she’d have been right in there.”

“She’s been through a lot as have you. Call me sometime this week. We need to talk.”

Bill nodded even as he headed after Cora, not seeing her at first. He ran to catch up with her, a hand on her arm stopping her.

“What now, Bill? Going to lecture me?” She was angry and wanting to fight with someone, who it was didn't really matter.

"No, I'm not. You're hurting. Why would I lecture a good friend in that situation?" He drew her with him to his car and tucked her inside, stopping with a hand on the closed door as he looked around. He could sense the encroaching danger, just couldn't see who it was.

Cora watched with interest as Bill's group of friends mingled in the park, a potluck supper underway with a planned baseball game after. Bill sat beside her on the bleachers, leaning forward as he spoke with Jonah and Candace sitting beside her. She had finally met all his friends and their wives, realizing how many of then she did know after all. They had made her feel welcome, a part of their group, but she still hesitated to get involved with them, not with whatever was hanging over her head.

Bill watched her face, seeing the conflicting emotions spreading across them before he reached for her hand and squeezed it. She looked down, then up at him, an unreadable look on her face. Before either could speak, Bill was called out to pitch.

Candace watched as Cora moved restlessly, her gaze shooting around.

"Cora?"

Cora's head spun at Candace's quiet voice. "I'm sorry, Candace. I feel someone watching me and I can't see whoever it is."

"I know that feeling. We all lived it unfortunately, but survived and became stronger because of it." She paused to gather up some of the plates and cups and bottles sitting round them. "Come on. We need to walk off that meal. Every time we get together, the meal outdoes the last one."

Cora rose as well, taking some of the debris from her. "How often do you get together?"

"We try for once a month. Not everyone can make every meal, but we get to as many as we all can. Today, everyone is here, which is nice." She paused, not quite sure how to continue, her words hesitant. "I'm glad you came with Bill. He needs you in his life."

Cora gave an unladylike snort. "I don't think so. We were friends in school, but time and life has intervened."

Candace nodded. "That it has, but both of you are wiser and have evolved into people who need one another. What you've lived through, what God has done in your lives, has brought you to this point." She dumped the debris in the garbage can and dusted off her hands. "Let's walk around the edge of the diamond. If we get too close, they'll try and involve us in the game and I don't think that's what you want."

Cora shook her head. "It's not. I can't run any more. I'm not allowed." She turned her head as she heard a small popping sound. "Do you hear that, Candace?"

Matthias had walked towards them, then shouted at them to run.

Candace took off, Cora hesitating, knowing that with whatever was coming, she wouldn't get out of the way in time. A concussion picked the two women and Matthias up and threw them forward. They landed heavily and lay still, the remains of the garbage container spread around them.

The men playing ball spun towards the commotion, then gloves, ball and bat flying, ran towards the three crumpled on the ground. Jonah and Larkin dropped besides their spouses. Bill reached for Cora, not wanting to touch her, afraid he had lost her too.

Andrew dropped to his knees on her other side and felt for a pulse. "She's alive, Bill. Help in on the way." He stood, his eyes searching for answers. He walked towards the remnants of the garbage container, sure he knew what had happened.

Josiah and Adam walked towards him, stern looks on their faces. "Andrew?"

"Yeah, Josiah?"

"What happened?"

"A bomb. But who knew Cora would be here?"

"You're sure it was meant for her?"

Andrew nodded. "Lily had just sent me a text that a death threat had come in against her. It also said Bill was a target too."

Adam sighed. "Not Bill. How do we keep him safe, him an officer and all?"

Andrew nodded. "I know. It's not as easy as it was with you all." He turned as he heard the sirens cut out as the emergency vehicles slid to a halt and calls could be heard from the responding officers and paramedics.

He walked back towards his friends, grateful to hear Matthias speaking and then Candace's voice. His eyes lit on Bill and he knew that Cora had not responded yet.

Andrew's hand on Bill's arm drew him up and out of the way as the paramedics, Ezra and Annie, worked on Cora. Compassion flowed through Andrew as he saw the look on Bill's face. *Yes, Lord, he has it bad, doesn't he? Protect his heart as You protect both of them. You're sending healing to Bill. Please heal Cora as well.*

Bill watched for a moment, then turned to Andrew, anger burning through him. "Who, Andrew?"

Andrew shook his head. "We just got a message in, just before that exploded, that Cora was a target of a death threat. So are you."

Bill stared at him, before his eyes went back to Cora. He watched as she was carefully placed on a backboard, neck collar in place, oxygen mask on her face, IV in her arm and then transported to the ambulance.

"I need to go with her."

Andrew's hand held him back. "No, what you need to do is find her parents and get them there."

Bill's head hung. Andrew was right. Cora was just a friend, even though he had begun to think of her as more than that. He nodded finally, reaching for his keys, before Andrew's hand once more stopped him.

"Let Silas drive you, Bill. I don't think you should be driving."

Bill studied Andrew's face before he nodded. "You're right. Where is he?"

"By your car. Madigan is heading to the hospital in theirs."

Three hours later, Bill paced the waiting room of the local hospital Emergency Department, waiting with Cora's parents on word about her. They had been back to see her but had been sent back out to wait.

Finally, he looked up as he heard the outside doors swish open and Andrew appeared, walking towards them. He nodded at the Brodies, then tilted his head away from them. Bill followed him down the hall towards the examination rooms.

"What do you know so far, Andrew?"

"That it was a bomb and it was meant to kill. Cora was the target. The thing is, how did they know she was there? How did they know to plant the bomb when all of us were around? The techs say it was likely detonated remotely, they're still working that through."

Bill ran his hands through his hair, one more time of many that night. "They're tracking her, somehow. But how? She wasn't driving. She said she had forgotten her phone. You have her rings."

Andrew nodded. "Is there another piece of jewelry that she wears?"

Bill turned to stare at him. "She has a locket. You don't think…" His voice died away.

Andrew nodded. "We'll need that. Stay put." He headed for the examination room where Cora was, coming back with all her jewelry, a watch, her locket and another ring.

"Do you recognize any of these that she's had for years?" Andrew held up the evidence bag he had tucked the jewelry into.

"The ring. It was a gift from her parents for her sixteenth birthday. The others, I don't know. You'd have to ask her parents. And she's said she doesn't always wear a watch. She never did when we were teens."

Bill turned as the stretcher bearing Cora was wheeled past him. He frowned at the fact she was still unconscious, seeing the cuts and bruises on her face and arms. His heart hurt for his friend but he grew angry that someone had hurt her. He sighed to himself. Anger wouldn't find the culprits. Lord, please heal her in all ways. She's hurting so bad. Not just from today. Bring back my friend. He paused in his prayer, finally acknowledging his feelings. He did love her, loved her with a passion he had not felt for Elizabeth, as much as he had deeply loved and cherished that lady, a passion for Cora in his heart that would never have risen had his beloved Elizabeth lived. He prayed hard that he wouldn't hurt his friend, ruin their renewed friendship.

Andrew watched the emotions flickering across Bill's face before he turned as a patrol officer approached and then waited for Andrew to walk towards him. A few minutes of quiet conversation and Andrew motioned for Bill to come with him.

"What's up, Andrew?"

"We're putting a guard on Cora tonight. There's one on you as well." Andrew held up his hand as Bill protested. "You were named as well, Bill, in the death threat. Lily's working on tracking where it came from, but isn't having much success."

Bill wasn't happy with that, but he knew Andrew had his best interests at heart.

He sighed, the sigh reaching way down inside him. "I guess you're right. Where do you want me?"

"For now, with Cora." Andrew laid a hand on Bill's shoulder. "She's hurt and I know you're hurting, too, because you couldn't protect her. Let me pray with you, Bill." He drew Bill off to the side to do just that.

Chapter 10

Cora moved, pain coursing through her body. She didn't know where she was or why she was hurting so badly. She cracked her eyes open, taking in the medical equipment and then the hospital room. Her eyes slid closed. Not again, dear Lord, please not again. I told You I never wanted to be in one of these rooms again.

A hand on hers brought her eyes open again as she looked first at the hand and then the man standing beside her. Bill stood there, a shadowed look on his face, stubble covering his jaw, an exhausted look around his eyes.

"Bill?" Her voice could barely be heard.

"Cora. You're awake. They didn't expect that until at least tomorrow. Your parents slipped home about an hour ago to get some rest." He looked over at the night sky he could see through the window before he reached to brush the hair from her face, then laid his hand gently on her cheek. "How are you feeling?"

"Sore. Please tell me I didn't hurt the knee again." Tears of pain gathered in her eyes.

"Your knee?"

She nodded and regretted it at the headache she felt. "I hurt it in a bad fall. I had surgery, but they couldn't totally fix it. That's why I can't run any more."

"I wondered. How long?" He watched as she shifted, pain flickering across her face before she hid it.

"Two, almost three years I guess. Nigel and I were hiking and I took a tumble." She looked up at his sudden silence. "Bill?"

"Was it an accident, Cora?" Bill's mind was working, trying to see what had actually happened.

"It was." Her voice died away, as her eyes slid closed. "Are you telling me you think it wasn't?"

"No, not that. I just wondered. How long had you been going out with Nigel at that point?"

"A year or so, I guess. It was just after he proposed. I know. A long engagement."

She studied her hands before laying her head back on the pillow, a deep sigh rising from within before she groaned with pain. "I can't do this, Bill. I need out of here. I can't stay in the hospital." Panic was beginning to rise.

"Cora. Look at me." When she didn't respond, his hands cupped her face and forced her to look at him. "I'm not saying he had anything to do with it. But Andrew needs to know this."

She nodded, her eyes sliding past him as the door slid open and a man entered. She frowned, not knowing him.

Bill spun to face the man, having seen the look of surprise and worry on Cora's face. He relaxed as he recognized the man.

"Jacob!" He reached to shake the hand of Jacob Wright, Elizabeth's father. "What brings you here?"

"I needed to talk to you. Is there somewhere we can talk in private?" Jacob's face showed his stress.

"Sure. Cora, this is Jacob Wright, Elizabeth's father. Jacob, this is Cora Brodie, a friend of many years."

Jacob nodded from where he stood, his eyes studying first Cora and then Bill, before he turned and walked from the room.

"Will you be okay if I leave?" Bill was worried about Cora.

"Go, Bill. I'll be fine." She watched as he turned at the door, his eyes searching hers, a look on his face she couldn't read before he left. Lord, I need out of here. I need to find out who is doing this. There has to be something in my photos or that I have that would tell me who.

She pushed herself up on the bed, reaching for the IV and pulling it, clamping the sheet over the blood seeping from her arm. She swung her feet over the edge of the bed, waiting until her head cleared before she rose and walked on tentative feet to the closet, finding her clothes and dressing as quickly as she could. She paused, leaning against the closet door to regain some strength. She crept to the door, pulling it open, watching as the officer assigned to her looked the other way before she slid out and was gone.

The man watched from the shadows as she slipped out the back door of the hospital and walked away, her steps hesitant as she moved forward. She finally found a taxi, taking it to her parents' home before she stood, looking up at the house, then moving to her car and driving away. She pulled over, sending a text to her mother she knew her mother would find in the morning. She needed time to sort this all out.

Bill stood in the doorway of Cora's hospital room, not seeing her, seeing the both the bathroom and closet doors open before he shook his head. She had made her escape while he had been talking with Jacob. He lightly fingered the envelope he had tucked into his back pocket before he turned to watch Andy, the patrol officer assigned to the door, searching the room.

"You won't find her, Andy." He gave a half grin at the look on Andy's face. "It's not your fault. She likely watched until you turned your head and then snuck out."

Andy shook his head. "I saw you leave but never saw her."

Bill laughed outright at that. "Don't worry. I'll explain it to Andrew. Search and see if you can find her. Then I'd check the security tapes for the back door."

"Back door?" Andy studied Bill, wondering at that.

"Back door. She's an old friend from years ago. That's what she would do, sneak out the back door." He turned, reaching into his pocket for his keys. "Call Andrew and then dispatch. Have them watch for her car. She's apt to be trying to get back to Oak City and her place. I'll try and find her."

Bill drove by the Brodie's, not seeing Cora's car, and sighed once more. Cora, what have you done? You're not up to that drive but I know you'll try. Lord, keep Your hand on the wheel of her car. Keep my lady safe. Bill didn't realize the way he had prayed, his thoughts on Cora and her safety.

Cora stood in her apartment, staring around. It was trashed, yes, it was trashed once again. She sighed. She wasn't up to anything tonight, other than crawling into her bed and falling asleep. It probably hadn't been a good idea to sneak out of the hospital. Her head was pounding. She paused. No, that was someone at the door. She quietly moved to peer through the peep hole, her head resting down against the door. Bill! How had he known where to find her? And at this time of the morning, if he kept knocking he'd wake up the senior man across the hall and she'd never hear the end of it.

Bill stood watching Cora stand in her doorway, assessing her. No, he thought, she's not in good shape. He finally moved towards her, forcing her back into the hallway and then closing and locking the door after himself.

"Don't say it, Bill!" Cora was ready for a fight.

"Say what? I'm concerned that you drove all this way when you're not well." He reached out a hand to steady her, before he looked around. "Wow! Temper tantrum already?"

She smacked his arm, earning herself a grin. "No, it was like this when I got here."

"They had time. Let me call it in. Meanwhile, you find somewhere to crash for a bit." He pointed to the kitchen. "In there. Put your head on the table and sleep. This will take a while."

He approached her a couple of hours later. She was sound asleep, her head pillowed on her arms, the blanket still around her shoulders that he had found for her. She hadn't stirred with the activity of the officers and crime scene techs working around the place. His hand rubbed her back for a moment before he moved past her. The officers had come and gone, not finding anything. He stood for a moment, hands resting on the kitchen counter, before he turned, gathering Cora into his arms and heading for her bedroom, tucking her in with a blanket over her before he closed the door and headed back to make coffee. He yawned, knowing he needed sleep, but wanting to start clearing up the mess.

Cora awoke, stiff and sore as she stretched, her eyes searching the room. She shot upright, wondering how she had managed to get back to her own place. She stood for a moment in the hallway, hearing soft movements, her heart racing before she saw Bill heading for the kitchen, mug in hand. He paused, turning as he sensed her, just standing and watching, assessing her.

"Bill?" Cora stepped into the living room, surprised to see it was tidy once more. "What did you do? What time is it?"

"About 7 or so. I let you sleep. You needed it." He approached, his head tilting to study her face, wincing at the bruises and the cuts, distress coursing through him at the stress she showed. "You didn't hear any of the activity around you last night."

She shook her head. "I didn't. I guess I was more tired than I thought. Why?"

"Why what?"

"Why did you do this?"

He shrugged. "It's what I do for friends." He stopped, his eyes raising to the ceiling as he bit his lower lip, not quite sure how to continue.

Cora brushed past him, her steps still unsteady as she walked through the apartment. Her bedroom had been the only not tossed, and she frowned at that.

"Why not the bedroom?" She turned too quickly, catching her balance with a hand to the door frame. Bill stood where she had left him, his eyes steady on her.

"Did they find what they were looking for?"

She shrugged. "I don't know what they were looking for?" Her voice raised sharply into a question. She sighed. "This is the second time this has happened here." She glanced at her wrist, missing her watch. "I need to speak with the superintendent. And where's my watch?"

"He's not there until 9. And Andrew has your watch." Bill reached out a hand, waiting as she eyed first it and then him. "Come on, Cora. You know me well enough to know I have your best interests at heart."

Cora studied Bill's face, seeing the caring and compassion he had always showed. She knew he had liked to tease and torment as his mother had put it, but he had a heart of gold and was there for his friends, no matter the cost. She reached for his hand, relishing the strength she found as his folded gently around hers and tugged her towards him and into one of his hugs.

"Come on. There's fresh coffee and I slipped out and found some food for us." He seated her, set the coffee and food in front of her, then slid into a seat, bowing his head to ask the blessing on their food and ask for safety for Cora. He sighed as he heard the doorbell ring, his hand on her arm keeping her seated as he rose

She heard the voices in the hallway, one angry, Bill's calm, before she went to see what was the issue. The building superintendent stood there, staring around.

"Ms. Brodie. The owners of the building want you out. Here's a check for all the rent you've paid."

"They can't do that." She was shocked, her eyes on the envelope, then on him.

"They have. Be out by noon today."

Bill stood in front of the door, hearing measured steps in the hallway nearing the door. "I don't think they can. They're breaking the lease and breaking the law. Miss Brodie will be in touch with a lawyer.

Meanwhile, there are some officers right outside the door who want to talk with you downtown."

The man paled, discomfort in his demeanour as he shifted uneasily from foot to foot. "I have nothing to talk to them about."

Bill shook his head as he stepped to one side and opened the door. "I think you do. The owners of this building are under investigation for many things, including money laundering and running drugs. For all we know, you're part of it. So, you will go with these nice officers. Miss Brodie will be out by midnight tonight. You will also be hearing from her lawyer as well as as many other city and legal departments as I can dream up to contact you." Bill watched as the man walked away with the two officers, one officer hanging back to briefly speak with Bill.

Cora snapped her mouth shut, anger building within her, at who, she still wasn't quite sure. She spun, heading for the kitchen, and heard Bill's soft footsteps behind her. Of course, he would be and he had taken off his shoes too.

Bill watched her closely as she struggled to find the words to tell him off and he wasn't prepared to let her do just that. The police chief, a cousin of sorts of Andrew's Phoebe, had been in touch and told him a mover was coming in shortly to start packing her up. Even without the eviction notice, he said she was part of their investigation and needed protection. Bill agreed.

He walked towards Cora, backing her up until she hit the wall behind her and then stood, hand on either side of her head, watching as she shrank back. He sighed. This was not going well. He dropped his hands from the wall, reaching for hers and leading her to the table. He made her sit and then reached to pour them both coffees before he sat beside her, gathering his thoughts and words.

"What time do we have to really be out by, Bill? And can he do this?"

Bill shook his head. "Legally, they can't kick you out this quick. But for your own safety, we need to move you and all your belongings."

"Then why do I have to?"

"For your own safety, for one thing. Another reason? If they keep coming back here, they'll be seen and someone will get hurt. The police here consider you part of their investigation now and want you kept safe. That's why there'll be a mover here in a short while, to pack you up and store your furniture. Your personal stuff and books will go wherever you want them to." He watched with compassion the emotions flickering across her face.

She finally sighed, dropping her head into her hands. "Why does it have to be me, Bill? What does God have against me?"

"God doesn't have anything against you, Cora. He uses people and circumstances to bring us back to Him, to bring others to justice. I've seen it so many times in the last few years."

She shook her head. "I just don't get it." She sighed and rose, heading for her bedroom. "I guess I should start packing." She stopped in the doorway, knowing Bill sat and watched her. "Thank you for what you're doing, Bill. I really do appreciate it." She disappeared from sight.

Bill sighed himself, knowing the battle hadn't been won with Cora, knowing she really didn't get how much in danger she was, even with the bomb going off yesterday. Was it only yesterday, he asked himself? He pulled out his phone as a text message chimed and frowned as he read it. What next, Lord? He rose and headed for the door, knowing the movers would be there as well as a team of off-duty officers Wesley had rounded up to help.

Four hours later, Cora stood in the empty apartment, her thoughts mixed. On one hand, she was glad to be out of there. Memories assailed her and she bit her lip to fight the tears. On the other hand, she was angry that she had to move. She felt an arm around her shoulders and leaned into Bill. He had always been able to read her emotions, even as a teenager.

"Doing okay?" His words were soft in her ear, his breath whispering across her cheek.

She nodded. "I'll get there. Now what, Bill? If I'm in that much of danger, how do I go back to Mom and Dad's?"

He hugged her tighter, his eyes on Wesley who stood watching them before Wesley pointed out the door. Bill nodded, before he leaned back to look down at his friend.

"Cora, we need to put you somewhere you'll be safe. Just where, we have no idea."

She stared up at him. "Just not Mom and Dad's. I couldn't bear it if something happened to them because of me."

"We know that. I have a little building at the back of my lot, accessible from the yard or the laneway behind my place. It's set up as a granny flat. It's yours for however long you need it. The security's good on it."

She watched as he walked her outside to the parking lot, stopping suddenly and staring around.

"Where's my car? And yours?"

He pointed. "Yours is on the flatbed tow truck. An officer has already left with mine."

"Just why is mine on there?" She spun, ready to fight, when she saw the couple walking towards them and then groaned. "Don't tell me. More friends?"

He nodded. "Leah, Joseph, I'd like you to meet Cora. That's her car you have there, Leah."

Cora stared at him, then at the lady he had introduced as Leah. "You're the driver?"

"I am." Leah grinned. "Dad has a tow company among other things and I'm one of the drivers. Joseph here works in security, so he's along for the ride today. He's also my husband." She grinned up at him before adding. "We had an adventure too, months ago. So we help when we can." She turned to Bill. "I'll drop the car off at the address you gave Dad."

"Thanks, Leah. We appreciate you getting up this early to help. Especially when you're on vacation."

"Not a problem, Bill. You'd do the same for us." With a quick wave, Joseph led his wife back to the truck, helping her up to the driver's seat before running around and climbing in himself.

"Just how many friends do you have that I don't know about?" Cora's disgruntled question made Bill laugh as he caught her hand and directed her to where Wesley was standing.

"Many, and all willing to help out."

He helped her into the back seat of the SUV then slid in beside her, Wesley finally sliding in on her other side. Cora was lost in thought for a few minutes until she looked up, surprised at seeing the brothers on either side of her. She glared at first one and then the other, her eyes shooting to the front as two more men slid into the front seats. Bill, watching her face, barely contained his grin, noting that Wesley didn't even try.

Cora turned, a glare on her face, to watch Bill, seeing his amusement, her eyes narrowing at it.

"What's going on, Bill?"

He nodded to the two men. "Our driver's name is Murphy. He works for Abe, our other companion, who has a security team. They offered to help out today."

"Help out, in how?" She saw the look Abe and Murphy exchanged and turned to glare first at Wesley, who nodded, and then Bill. "Do I really need this much protection?"

"You might and you might not. We're not taking any chances, Cora. After what you've had happen to you the last few days, we need to keep you safe. Abe will see us safely home. He has someone running the security system at my place to make sure it's more than adequate."

Cora slumped back against the seat, arms folded across her chest, a frown in place. She finally spoke. "Your SUV's the wrong colour."

Abe turned, an eyebrow raised in question. "The wrong colour? I thought black was fine."

"It should be white." Her stare turned to Murphy as he shouted with laughter, causing the other three men to stare at him.

"Good one, Cora. I'll need to remember that the next time I buy a vehicle." Murphy's enjoyment at her statement was evident.

Abe, Wesley and Bill exchanged puzzled glances until Murphy took pity on them. "She thinks we're riding up on a black charger when it should be white."

The men laughed, breaking the tension in the vehicle. Cora settled back against Bill, a smirk on her face. Finally she had gotten the upper hand with Bill.

Bill's arm around her tightened as she laid her head on his shoulder and then drifted off, the hum of the men's conversation fading. Bill listened for a while before his head went back and he too slept. Wesley studied the sleeping couple, then turned his attention back to Abe and the advice and suggestions he was giving. Wesley knew how hard it was going to be to keep these two safe and that worried him. He finally took his worry to the Lord and prayed for his brother and his lady.

Chapter 11

*C*ora roused as she sensed the car stop and rubbing at her eyes, looked around. Wesley, Abe and Murphy had all exited the vehicle and were searching around Bill's home. Bill was still asleep, his arm tight around her and she had to push at it to get him to move it. She sat upright, her eyes on her friend, as he too roused, a smile appearing on his face as he saw her.

"You slept."

She nodded. "I did. And so did you." She stared out the window. "Now what, Bill? How long do I hide?"

He stretched, then pushing open the door, stepped out and reached back for her hand, not releasing it when she stood beside him. "I hope for not too long. We need to keep you safe, Cora. They've proven they're after you."

"But I don't get why, Bill. That's the thing. I don't have anything that they want."

"Not that you know of." He turned and pointed to the little house he had told her she could use. "All your personal effects are in there."

She still hesitated. "I don't think I'm the one they're after."

Bill gave a growl of disagreement, causing her eyes to shoot to his before he caught her arm and pulled her with him to his office, where he shoved her down into his desk chair and booted up his computer. She made to rise and he shoved her back down.

"Sit. I want to show you something." His eyes raised to the doorway where the other three men stood, concern on their faces. "I want to show you exactly what happened that day."

Her face paled and she shook her head. "I know exactly what happened."

Bill stared at her, then shook his head even as he brought up the enhanced video. "No. You think you do. But you don't. You haven't see this." He played it for her, watching her intently, seeing her distress.

"I don't see anything other than what I remember."

Bill went back on the video, slowing it down even more, then stopped it at one point, his finger stabbing at the monitor, anger in his voice. "Right there. See that? He's not looking at Lock. He's looking directly at you, knife out, ready to stab you. You moved, Lock moved with you right into the way of the knife. If you hadn't moved, you'd be the one dead."

Cora sat back, horror on her face, as she reached to replay the moment, before burying her head in her arms. Sobs shook her body as the realization. Bill's hand rested on her shoulder before he turned and walked away, brushing by the men standing there, and heading the back door. After a few moments, he heard the door open and close and felt the presence of someone beside him.

"She didn't know?" Abe's voice was quiet as he spoke.

Bill shook her head. "No. She thought Lock was the target all along. Now, I have to deal with that as well as everything else going on."

"How much longer are you off?"

"Three weeks or so. I don't think it's going to be enough time, though, Abe. Something tells me it's going to drag on and on." Bill was frustrated.

"It can, or it can't. It depends on how anxious they are to find whatever it is she has. And she has something, whether she realizes it or not."

"I know she does. He put it somewhere in her place. My fear is that we've brought it with us and without knowing what it is, we can't find it."

He turned as he heard a sound behind him and found Cora standing there. Abe excused himself even as Cora walked towards Bill.

"What is it I'm supposed to have, Bill? That's my question. No one seems to know."

"I don't know either, but it's something pretty strong or meaningful to them." He sighed, reaching to pull her into a hug, his chin resting on her head. "We'll need to search through your things again, I think. It's there somewhere."

He felt her nod and then yawn. "I know, Bill, and I don't like it." She pulled back, not looking at him, not seeing the emotions playing out on his face. "I'm heading for the cottage as you call it. I'll see you in the morning."

He watched her walk away and then close the door behind her before he turned back to the house. Abe, Murphy and Wesley had left while the two were out back. He walked through the house, locking up. It was still early but it had been a long couple of days and he was exhausted.

Bill sat away from the box he had been sorting through, leaning back on his hands to watch Cora. She had pulled her hair back into a pony tail from which it was escaping as she concentrated on the box she was searching. She blew out a breath and looked up at him.

"What exactly are we looking for again?"

He laughed. "I have no idea. I thinking a thumb drive or something like that."

She nodded. "That makes sense. Andrew has the one I found earlier in my box of stuff." She paused, her eyes searching through the mess in her living room until she found what she was looking for. She rose, her hand reaching for the statue of an eagle. "He gave me this about a month before he died. I never liked it. It just didn't seem like a gift you should give someone who doesn't like this kind of clutter."

Bill rose and went towards her, reaching to take the statue from her. "This is interesting. Did he say anything when he gave it to you?"

She shook her head. "It just appeared one day. I always assumed it was from him."

Bill froze, his eyes tracing from her to the statue. "Do you mind?" He pointed to the statue.

"What do you have in mind?" She grew quiet as he put a finger to his lips and then left the cottage, Cora on his heels.

Bill headed for his garage and his workshop, setting the statue down and studying it, finally reaching for a hammer. He raised an eyebrow at Cora, who nodded. One swift blow of the hammer shattered the statue. Bill sorted through the pieces, finding the thumb drive he expected but also a key. Then his hand stilled as he found something totally unexpected. A GPS device, he thought. Lock would have put it there to track this. He searched the device, then bagged it, knowing he would have a trip to see Andrew that day. He gathered up the debris from the statue and bagged it as well. He approached Cora and stood, his hands on her arms until she looked up at him, an unreadable look on her face.

"We need to go see Andrew. Go, get your purse or whatever you need." He watched as she hesitated and then nodded before walking away. Lord, I have no idea how to keep this lady safe. Guide me here, please.

Andrew looked up from his desk as he heard Bill's voice and sighed. Bill shouldn't be here, he thought, before he took a look at the budget he was working on and then threw down his pen, rising to find Bill. He stood for a moment, watching as Bill introduced Cora to the officers and staff in the building, his arm tight around her. Andrew shook his head. Bill, what have you done? You've just staked your claim and interest in her, bringing her in like this. You have never dated that we know of and now this. Andrew knew he'd be fielding many questions about Bill, given how close they were as friends.

Bill turned as Andrew approached, finished his conversation and then led Cora towards Andrew, pointing towards a conference room. Andrew nodded and headed that way.

Bill sat the bags on the table, then stood in front of Cora, his eyes searching her face before she nodded. He gently pushed her into a chair, then turned to Andrew.

"I think we found what they were looking for. Lock had given Cora an eagle statue, which we destroyed this morning. We found a thumb drive, a key, and a GPS unit.”

“That’s an interesting combination. I’ll have the lab run the GPS and see what they can tell us about that. They’ll look at the thumb drive. Did you take a look at it?”

Both Bill and Cora shook their heads. “I headed right here with it.” Bill ran a hand through his hair. “We just have to figure out where the key goes.”

Cora rose and approached the table, picking up the key. “It’s a storage locker key, isn’t it? I still have the lease going on the apartment where Nigel lived and it has a storage area in the basement. I suspect this would fit it.”

Bill and Andrew shared a look. “You never told us you still had the apartment, Cora.” Andrew’s face grew stern. “It could hold important information.”

She shook her head. “The apartment is empty. I cleared it out about six months ago and gave everything away. I hadn’t had the heart to go into the storage locker.” She raised her eyes to the men. “I guess I have to, don’t I?”

Bill nodded, not looking at Andrew. He could feel Andrew’s agitation at Cora’s lack of concern. "We'll head there today, if you like, or tomorrow morning."

She sighed. "Tomorrow, I think, early." She stared at Bill. "How many more people are you going to drag along with us?"

Bill smirked. "I'll let you know tomorrow. I don't think we should go on our own. Wesley's not available."

Andrew watched as Bill worked it through, finally speaking. "Ask Abe, Richard, or Don if one of them or some of their team can go with you. I don't like you two going on your own."

Bill nodded as he looked up at Andrew. "I'll do that." He sighed as his phone chimed. "Wesley. He's available for tomorrow morning. Does that work, Cora?"

"It does. I might as well clear out the storage locker as well. The lease runs out in about six weeks."

Andrew and Bill exchanged glances, each knowing the other was wondering why Cora had never cleaned out the locker when she cleaned out the apartment.

Bill caught Cora's hand as he turned towards the door. "I'll let you know what I find, Andrew. Expect me to call sometime tomorrow afternoon."

"I'll hold you to that." Andrew stood, arms crossed as he watched the couple walk away, turning his head slightly as he heard Lily stop beside him.

"Andrew, who is she? Is she good enough for our Bill?"

Andrew gave a quiet smile but before he could reply, Sam spoke up from Lily's other side.

"Draw in the claws, Lily. Bill and Cora have been friends since before high school. They were part of a group that hung around together. We were surprised they didn't become a couple when they graduated, but they both went their separate ways." Sam shared a look with Andrew.

"But what did Bill mean when he said if and when he married again, Andrew? He's never said anything about being married." Lily stared up at her chief, a question on her face.

Andrew caught the same look on Sam's face before he spoke quietly. "Bill was married just after his junior year at college. His wife was killed about six months later." He pointed towards the door where the couple had disappeared. "And somehow Elizabeth's death is connected to Cora and the man she thought she was married to."

The two officers stared at the door, then after Andrew as he walked away back to his office before exchanging glances.

Chapter 12

Cora stared at the man walking towards Bill's vehicle the next morning, not recognizing him. She watched as Bill slid from behind the wheel and approached him. Then a gurgle of laughter bubbled up. It was Wesley. No, she hadn't recognized him, dressed as he was in faded jeans, tight T-shirt, work boots, carpenter's belt, dark-framed glasses, and hard hat. What was up, she wondered?

Bill opened her door and pulled her out, leading her towards the building, Wesley following slowly behind them. He shook his head as she went to ask something, reaching instead for the key she held.

"Not now, Cora. We'll explain once we're done."

"I'm sure you will." Laughter still underlined her voice. "The storage unit is this way."

"Hey! Wait! Can you hold the door for me?" Wesley's voice carried to them, and Bill turned, a frown on his face. "Thanks, man. I thought I'd be standing out here all morning, waiting for someone to let me in."

"I'm not sure I should be letting you in." Bill's frown stayed in place as Cora looked between the two, biting her lip to keep from laughing, before she stepped inside and headed for the stairs to the basement.

"Oh. Wow! It looks as if we're heading the same way! This is great!" Wesley followed them, his demeanour that of a worker, his eyes not missing much.

Bill tried hard to keep a straight face, not looking at Cora as he followed her down the stairs and to the storage locker she stopped in front of. He reached for the key, his fingers gripping hers tightly for a moment, before he turned the key in the lock and opened the door. A light switched on as he did so.

"That's something." He looked around the small area, before he entered, Cora on his heels.

"I'll watch for you two. If the door closes, stay quiet." Wesley pulled out his clipboard and tape measure and began to work around some of the other units. He heard footsteps heading down the stairs and quickly slid over and shut the door behind

Bill and Cora quietly before he headed across the hall to measure one of the other units.

He stood, back to the stairs, listening to the steps coming closer, but ignoring them. A tap on his shoulder had him throwing up his hands, pencil and tape measure flying through the air as he gave a suppressed cry before spinning around, eyes wide in pretended fright, to confront the men standing back from him, shock on their faces.

"What are you doing, man? Don't you know better than to sneak up on a person? You just scared me out of a year's growth." Wesley leaned back against the storage room door Bill and Cora were behind, hand to his chest, as he gave exaggerated breaths.

The two men stared at him and then one another before the shorter, more rotund one spoke, his tall thin companion watching.

"We're looking for a man and woman. They came down this way."

"Nope. Nobody here but me and now you and maybe a few spiders." Wesley pretended to swat at a cobweb. "They're multiplying down here you know, those spiders."

The men moved back, heading for the stairs. "You're absolutely sure?"

Wesley nodded, his hand tapping on the door. "Yep - just me. No one else in the hallway, now is there? Where would they be hiding if they were down here?"

The man looked around him. "In a storage area."

"The doors are all locked. Try them and see." He prayed the man didn't take him up on that.

Bill hugged Cora tight to him as he pulled her into a small alcove in the storage unit. He knew Wesley would open the door for him shortly. There hadn't been much in the unit, just a small cardboard box. Cora had been surprised at that.

Cora laid her head on Bill's chest, laughter shaking her body as they listened to Wesley outside. She raised her head to speak, but Bill's finger on her mouth kept her silent, a grin on his face as he too listened to his brother.

Wesley waited for a moment, then sprang to open the door, motioning them to come out and head for the back entrance. They had just disappeared from sight when he heard footsteps on the stairs again. He moved to a door away from where Bill and Cora were heading, clipboard in hand as he noted figures down, whistling off key. He ignored the steps coming towards him until he felt a tap on his shoulder.

Once more giving a shriek, he let his hands fly up and the clipboard sailed over his head, catching the taller of the two men in the forehead before clattering to the floor. The man yelled in pain as Wesley spun around. Wesley watched, amusement lurking in his eyes, as the man rubbed at the red spot on his forehead.

"I just told you not to do that. Now see what you've done?" He swiped up his clipboard in anger and brushed by the men. "I'm going to have to have a chat with the boss. I can't work in conditions like this. Interruptions. Scares. Obnoxious people." He stormed up the stairs and shoved through the doors, heading for the truck he had borrowed for the day. Bill's car was gone. He had arranged for that. Heading around to the back of the building in his truck, he slowed just enough for Bill to yank open a door, shove Cora inside with the small box and jump in himself, before he picked up speed and drove away. He watched with amusement as he saw the two men running out the back door, looking around for him.

Cora could no longer contain her laughter, and the musical sound of it filled the truck cab. Bill joined in as Wesley just grinned at them.

"Did you get what you were after?" His question sobered them somewhat.

"We did. There was only the one box, which I was surprised at." Cora stared at it. "It doesn't seem very suspicious, but I don't want to open it."

"We'll take it back to the department and let the techs have a go at it, if you want." Bill turned his head to watch her.

"No. I need to open it. I have no idea what he would have put in it."

Wesley and Bill exchanged glances before Wesley headed for the department building he worked out of. "Let me take you to the department. I'll set you up there. I don't think it's a good idea to take it to your home."

"No, not likely. Where's my car?"

Wesley just grinned as he handed over the visitor's badges and pointed to a room down the hall. "Lily's taken it back to your place. We'll get you two home." He flipped on lights as he entered the room, turning as Bill and Cora followed him, Sam on their heels.

"Sam?" Bill shouldn't have been surprised to see a fellow officer.

"Andrew sent me. He thought you might need protection or something."

Bill watched Cora's face as she stared at the box before looking up at Wesley, who nodded and left, taking Sam with him.

"Cora?" When she looked up, an unreadable look on her face, he spoke again. "I'll be right outside the door. Call me if you need me."

She finally nodded. Bill hesitated, then dropped a kiss on her cheek before he walked out, closing the door behind him. Cora stood, staring after him, hand on her cheek, wonder in her eyes. That was Bill who had just done that? Her eyes softened as her heart finally warmed. Yes, Lord, I hear You. Time to heal and move on. This box should be the final thing, I'm hoping.

She stared at the box, not ready to open it, but knowing she had to. Her fingers reluctantly pulled at the dried tape, peeling it back, before she took a deep breath and opened the flaps.

She stared down into the box, seeing Lock's writing on an envelope on the top. She removed it, her hands shaking as she did so. She reached in and pulled out the journals she found, counting them. Twelve, she thought. That's odd. Then, she realized they had years engraved on them. One for each year, up until the previous year. What was the meaning of this, she wondered?

She opened the envelope, finding just a small piece of paper with the words directing her to turn the journals over to a man she didn't know. No explanation. No apologies. She frowned, staring down at the paper and then the journals. She turned as the door opened, and Bill entered, a question on his face.

Cora turned her gaze back to the paper she had laid on the table, her hand flat on it, her thumb rubbing back and forth, an unreadable look on her face. Now what, Lord? She asked. If this man is a criminal, I can't turn this over to him. I have no idea who he is anyway or how to find him. I just want this over.

Bill perched on the edge of the table, his eyes searching her face before he followed the track of her thumb. He reached finally to still her hand motions, his hand warm and strong on hers.

"Cora?"

She could hear the unspoken question but didn't respond right away. She finally handed him the paper without saying anything, waiting until he read it.

A frown in place, Bill looked between the paper and her. "Do you know this man?"

She shook her head, her eyes distressed. "I have no idea who he is. I just know I'm not tracking him down and turning those over to him." She pointed at the journals, and Bill shifted so he could see them, another frown on his face.

"What are they?"

She shrugged. "I have no idea. I have not looked at them, nor do I want to. Take them to Andrew if you have to. I want nothing to do with them."

Bill reached for her and cradled her into a hug, his arms strong and tight around her. "We can do that today, Cora. We'll get them away from you."

She nodded. "Please. I just want to move on and I can't. He just keeps popping up every time I turn around. I'm tired of it." She leaned back, her eyes studying her friend. "What's in this for you, Bill?"

"I get to help a dear friend, someone I cherish very much, someone I want to get to know much better." He didn't realize his heart was in his eyes as he studied her.

Cora drew a deep breath, knowing that this was a defining moment for them both. She had to handle it right. If she didn't she lost a good friend. "Just what are you saying, Bill?"

"That I think we might make a couple. I would like to explore that possibility."

She finally nodded, then pushed away from him. "Let me think about it, okay?"

He opened his mouth to respond as the door opened and Wesley entered, a concerned look on his face. Bill watched Cora closely, then said in a low voice, "I'm comfortable with that. I would like to date you, Cora, but only when and if you're ready."

She shot him a glance, then nodded in a grateful manner, even as she turned to Wesley. She frowned at the look on his face.

"Bill. Cora. They knew you were in that building today. Lily was driving Bill's car back to Elmton and someone tried to run her off the road. They backed off when they realized it wasn't you, Bill."

Bill stood and began to pace. "I never dreamed they'd go after Lily. How'd they know we were there?"

"I suspect they were staking out the building, watching for you two to show up." Wesley turned to stare back at the door. "Sam's getting ready to head home. Do you want to ride with him or I can send you home in a patrol vehicle with an escort?"

"What vehicle does Sam have?"

"One of your SUVs. He can hide you two in the back until you're out of town. They won't see you." He nodded to the journals. "Pack those up and take them with you. Our department doesn't need to see them. As far as our chief is concerned, you didn't bring anything in here that he needs to know about."

Bill nodded as he turned to Cora, finding that she was standing beside him. She had dumped the journals back into the box and held it out for him.

"Let me get you a duffel bag or backpack for that, Bill. It won't be as obvious I hope. Then I'll take you out the back way. Sam's parked just behind the building."

Cora grasped Bill's hand tight as she followed him. This was far from over, she thought, and grew angry. How had she been such a fool, she wondered?

Chapter 13

As they approached Elmton, Bill sat up straighter, his eyes on Cora who had drifted off to sleep, her head on his shoulder, her hand tight in his. Sam had kept an eye on the couple and the road as he drove, feeling confident they hadn't been followed, but wondering just how far their feelings for each other went.

"Can you let us off at Ev's diner and then find Andrew to pass on the journals?" Bill's eyes were watchful as he scanned his hometown and then turned his attention to Cora. He touched her face with the back of his fingers to wake her as Sam parked behind the diner. "Come on, sleepyhead. Time to wake up."

Cora stirred, her hand pushing against Bill's chest as she shoved herself upright and brushed her hair back from her face. She frowned at him before giving a small smile.

"Where are we?"

"At Ev's. Sam's dropping us here and taking the journals to Andrew. Andrew will have Lily and the techs go through them and track down the name on that paper. You don't have to worry about them any more."

She nodded, then reached for the door, out of it and into the diner before either Sam or Bill could react.

"You have your hands full there, Bill." Sam watched with compassion as Bill stood for a moment watching Cora before he turned back.

"I know. She doesn't realize it's not over."

"She knows. She's just refusing to let them win. She was like that in high school."

Bill stared at Sam, not quite sure what he meant.

"You never saw it, did you? She hid a lot of insecurity. I saw it because I wasn't as close to her as you are."

Bill finally nodded, then pointed to the road. "Get out of here, Sam, before they see you. Tell Andrew to call me if he needs us."

Sam watched Bill walk away, then sighed. He had no idea where these two were heading.

Bill slid into the booth beside Cora, causing her to frown at him.

"There's a seat on the other side, Bill." When he didn't move, she thumped around on the seat to stare at him. "Bill?"

"I want to sit here, Cora, not just to protect you. I really do want to date you. Can we consider this a first date?"

She threw up her hands. "Bill! At this time? You decide you want to date?" Her words had a bit of a bite to them, causing him to grin at her, then at Ev as she stopped by their booth.

"Bill. You haven't been in this week yet." Ev was Andrew's aunt and kept track of all his friends.

"No, I haven't had a chance." He watched as Ev recognized Cora.

"Cora! How good to see you, my dear. I've missed you." Ev leaned past Bill to hug her. "Don't tell me."

Bill started to laugh as he nodded. "Sorry, Ev."

She shook her finger at him. "You weren't supposed to have an "adventure" too, Bill. You're supposed to solve them." Then she sighed. "But then Andrew wasn't either."

Bill laughed even harder as Cora swatted him before smiling at Ev.

"I'd like one of your BLTs, Ev. And a coffee."

Ev looked at Bill who shrugged. "Your usual, I suppose?"

She walked away as Cora watched. Bill had his eyes on the parking lot, a frown on his face. They had followed them, it seemed. Now how did they know they were here?

"Bill?" Cora's voice broke through his thoughts. "Is someone out there?"

He nodded. "There is." He threw her a look. "Let's eat. Then we plan."

"Plan?" She looked up with a word of thanks as Ev set their plates in front of them.

"We plan. First, we say our prayers."

He grinned at her once more as he reached for her hand before he said a blessing on their food.

Three hours later, Bill stood on his back deck, eyes searching the yard. Someone had been there, he felt their presence. They hadn't made it inside the house, he knew, his alarm system was too good. He pulled out his phone as it chimed and frowned.

"Silas?"

"Bill? How are you?" Silas' voice held concern.

"I'm doing okay, I guess. But that's not why you're calling."

"It is. We haven't talked for a while. I can see the burn-out happening to you. What can I do for you?"

"Solve this with Cora?" Bill grinned as Silas laughed, just as he knew he would. "Seriously, though, I don't know. I'm in new territory here, Silas, and have no idea which way to go."

"Trust in the Lord, my friend. He has both of you in the hollow of His hand. Remember that." Silas paused before he continued. "Have you ever talked to anyone about your wife?"

Bill sighed. "I have, thanks, Silas. Years ago. Now, it really doesn't seem to make that much difference. I know she's gone and I need to move on. It's hard." He spun as he heard a sound from the front of the house and ran that way. "Silas, call the fire department. Someone just set my garage on fire."

Silas found Bill an hour later, standing on the sidewalk across from his house, his arms around Cora, as they watched the activity. The house was scorched but safe. Madigan squeezed Silas' hand as she walked with him.

Bill turned his head, his eyes on Silas and then Madigan. "Should have known you two would turn up."

"Of course we would. Cora, are you okay?" Madigan reached to hug Cora as Bill stepped back.

"No. I'm not. I'm so angry right now." She looked at Madigan in shock as she began to laugh.

"I'm sorry, Cora. That is just so you. Why don't you do a story on yourself? Would your editor allow it?"

Cora mulled that over, slowly nodding. "I'm sure he would. I'll talk to him." She ignored the looks Bill was shooting her way and turned and walked away from him.

"Did she really just do that?" Bill stood, hand on his head, as he watched her.

"She did, my friend." Silas grinned as he watched Cora pace down the street. "She needs some time, Bill. Let me try and talk with her."

"I don't think that will work, Silas. She has a trust issue where ministers are concerned." He sighed, knowing he would have to tell Silas what he meant. "This is confidential, just between us. She told me she's talked to ministers in the past and they have not kept what she's said confidential. That's a huge issue with her." Silas nodded before he walked away, Bill's eyes following him, Madigan's heart raised in prayer.

Silas caught up with Cora as she stood, arms folded across her abdomen, under the shade of a huge oak tree. She watched him, wary as to what he wanted.

"Are you sure you're okay, Cora?" Silas watched her closely, seeing the change that had come over her in the last few minutes. She's terrified, Lord, and how do I reach through that?

She shook her head. "Not really. I wanted, no, needed to get away from Bill. He'll get hurt if I stay around him."

Silas shook his head. "No, that's not true, Cora. He's in as much danger as you are. Somehow, Elizabeth and you have been linked by these people. Why, I have no idea. I don't think even Andrew has a complete handle on it yet."

She paced, not liking what she was hearing but knowing Silas spoke the truth. "So, where do we go from here, Silas?" She turned, her eyes seeing Bill watching from where she had left him before he turned to answer a call.

Silas shrugged. "I have no idea, Cora. Madigan and I had it different from you." He thought back on what they had gone through and shuddered. "But I do know that God is there for you, every step of the way."

Cora spun back to face him, a look he couldn't read on her face. "Now, that's what I don't get. I don't get that He is there. I don't see Him or feel Him."

"He's there, Cora. Just like this breeze. You can't see it, but you know it's there." Silas' head turned as he heard a vehicle slow and then stop, doors opening and closing. He moved to stand in front of Cora, not recognizing the men.

Cora peeked around him, a frown on her face. No, she didn't know these men, but they seemed familiar, somehow.

"What do you want?" Silas' voice was stern as he watched the men walk across the grass towards them.

"Her." The shorter of the men moved to walk around him, but Silas moved into his path.

He didn't hear the man approaching from behind him but felt the blow to his head, knocking him down and out. His sprawled body got barely a look before the second man moved towards Cora as well. Cora backed away, until she could back no further, tight to the oak tree.

"Where is it?" The shorter man reached for her neck, his hands closing around it. "We want what he gave you."

"I don't have anything left. I've given it all away." Her voice died away as the fingers tightened and her face was shoved to the side, the rough bark scraping it.

"You do. You were at his apartment today. What did he leave there?"

"I don't have anything of his. Not a thing." Cora struggled, finally getting her hands up to scratch at the man's face. His hold on her broke, and she screamed as she scrambled away from him.

Bill spun from where he stood talking to the fire captain as he heard the scream and then took off on a run, heading for his lady. Officers ran after him as a couple headed for their vehicles. Andrew threw his car into park and ran as well, not quite sure what was happening but he knew it involved Bill and Cora.

Cora's arm was caught by the taller of the men and she was pulled towards their vehicle, struggling the whole while. The man didn't see Silas stagger to his feet and throw himself at him until he felt the impact of Silas' body hitting him and taking him to the ground. Cora broke free and ran towards Bill's house, the shorter man running after her, sliding to a stop as he saw the men running towards him. He spun and ran for his vehicle, finding it blocked in by patrol cars. He stopped, hands raising slowly as he was ordered to do before dropping to his knees, cursing the woman for getting away and the man who interfered.

Bill caught Cora in his arms, holding her tight as she struggled until she relaxed, feeling safe in his arms, her head buried against him, finally hearing his calm quiet words of reassurance. Andrew motioned for Bill to take her back to his place even as he moved past them to where the officers were waiting with their prisoners. He took a look at Silas and sighed.

"Silas, what did you go and do?"

Silas gave a tight grin as he rubbed the back of his head and grimaced. "Nothing I planned, that's for sure. I told Bill I'd talk to Cora, caught up with her here, and then everything just went black." He turned, glaring at the men behind him. "The tall one. He's the one that slugged me from behind."

Andrew nodded, watching for a while as officers combed the area for evidence, his eyes on the men in separate cars. He spoke quietly to one of the officers, then motioning to Silas, turned to head back to Bill's.

"I want you to stay away from Cora and Bill until we have your statements. From what I gather, it won't take long." Andrew watched as Madigan ran to her husband, her eyes searching his face.

"I'm fine, Madi. Just a bump on the head." Silas caught her tight, the sight of her making him thankful he hadn't been hurt worse. He nodded to where Cora sat on a neighbouring house's porch, Bill tight to her side. "Cora's the one I'm worried about."

"What happened?"

Andrew shook his head at Madigan. "Not yet, Mads, not until he gives his statement and I have him checked out by the paramedics. Then, you two can talk." His hand on Silas' arm, he led him to a patrol officer, Madigan trailing after them.

Andrew walked towards Cora, nodding to Ezra, one of the paramedics, to follow him. Cora had just finished her statement, her hand shaking as she took the bottle of water Ezra handed her. She looked up at Andrew, a shuttered look in her eyes.

"Cora?"

"What?" She sighed. "Sorry, Andrew. This has not been a good day." She took a drink of water, her hand shaking too much to put the cap back on and Bill reached to steady her hands.

"No, I guess it hasn't been. Let Ezra take a look at you." He grimaced as he saw the red marks on her neck and the scrapes on her face before he stepped back to speak with the officer.

Bill stood beside him, anger radiating from him. "What now, Andrew? How do we keep her safe?"

"I don't know, Bill. We've been through this so many times lately I think I've run out of ideas. Do you have any?"

Bill considered that, an idea forming in his mind. "I might have an idea, but I need to work it through first, and then talk to Cora.

As soon as I have something definite, I'll call you."

Andrew stared at him. "We need to do something soon, Bill, or Cora won't survive, and you know that. Neither will you. They'll take either one of you as soon as an opportunity presents itself. Today proves that."

Cora pushed Ezra's hands away from where he was dressing her scrapes and stood, hands on her hips, glaring at the two men. "No one makes any decision without my input, got that?" Bill raised a hand to cover a smile as Andrew stared at her, his eyes narrowed.

"If we have time, we'll welcome you to do just that, Cora. But if it comes to it and your safety and the safety of those around you is compromised, I'll make the necessary decision to put you somewhere safe."

Bill exchanged an amused glance with Ezra behind Cora's back before he laid an arm around her shoulders. "Back down, Cora. Andrew's the police chief, remember? He can put you into protective custody as a material witness if he so chooses."

"He'd have to find me first." Cora was not backing down, her eyes tracing past the men to where the patrol vehicles had sat. "I can disappear and trust me, no one would ever find me."

"That we don't want you to do. There are other people you need to consider, besides yourself. Bill, here. Your parents. Your employer. Do you not think they won't go after any one of them to get to you, to say nothing of your friends?" Andrew tamped down his anger, and prayed for the words to reach through to her.

Chapter 14

$\mathcal{C}$ora stared at her computer screen, not seeing the images on it, but instead the face of the man who had assaulted her three days previous. She frowned. Something about him seemed familiar. She searched through the photos she had printed, then turned to her backups, finally finding the one she wanted.

She scrolled through the images, her hand stilling on the mouse as she saw the one she wanted, her heart sinking within her. She did know him, just didn't know who he was. He had briefly appeared one day as a friend of Lock's, but she hadn't spoken to him, had barely given him a glance, her attention that day focused on the rock formations she was studying and photographing for her travelogue. She sighed and reached to print the photo, knowing she had to make a trip to see Andrew.

Then, she reached for his business card and sent the photo to him in an email, forgetting about it once she had sent it, her attention going back to her next travelogue.

She finally sat back, happy with her video, and sent it on to her employer. It had been a change of pace for her, showing off her home town. She knew Andrew and Bill would not be happy that she had chosen to do just that at this time but she didn't regret it. Maybe, she thought, just maybe it will bring it all out into the open. She was so ready to have this all over and be able to go on with her life.

She reached for her phone, muted as was her custom when she was working, and smiled at the number of times Bill had called or sent a text message. The last one sounded rather frantic, she thought. She sent off a text in reply, then rose, stretching. She had moved back to her parents' for the duration, she thought, but realized she wasn't happy there. She searched for her father's newspaper and hunted out the apartment to rent ads.

She paused as she heard the doorbell and turned that way. No one should be here, she thought, fright winging its way through her. Did she answer it or not? She crept to the door, looking out the side window. Madigan stood there, looking around.

"Madigan?" Cora's question had Madigan turned towards her, a big smile on her face.

"Cora? How are you today?"

Cora stepped back to let Madigan in. "I'm okay, I guess. Come on back to the kitchen. I was just about to find something to eat. I worked through lunch."

"I don't need anything." Madigan slid into a chair at the table and accepted the mug of tea Cora set in front of her. "I came to see you, not to eat."

"It's a rule here. We feed everyone who walks through the door." Cora set a plate of fruit bread down between their places and then sat herself with her cup of coffee. "Why are you really here, Madigan?"

"You needed a friend. That's what God told me today when I was praying for you." She reached to grasp Cora's hand as Cora studied her face. "What is really going on, Cora? I sense you're anxious but you've made a decision."

Cora sighed. "I have. I can't continue to live here at Mom and Dad's." She flicked the paper. "I was searching out apartments to rent when you rang the doorbell."

"Living on your own is a decision you're comfortable with, at this time?" When Cora nodded, Madigan sat back, a smug look on her face. "I know just the place. A friend has an apartment in the upper half of her house that just vacated. You two would get along just fine."

"Would she be comfortable with me there, given the danger I could bring?"

Madigan nodded. "She would be. It's Lily's sister."

"Lily? As in the detective?" Cora sat back. "No. I don't think so. That would cause problems with Bill."

"Really? All right, then. I have another friend, an older lady, who has an apartment or rather half a house she'd rent you." Madigan stood. "Come on. I know she's home today. Let's go see her."

An hour later, Cora sat back in Madigan's car, satisfied.

"I like her. And the place suits me so well." She turned to watch Madigan as she drove. "How did you know?"

"Know what?"

"Know to come today and that I needed some place to live."

Madigan shrugged as she pulled off at a small coffee shop and pointed to it. "Let's go get a coffee and talk."

Cora hesitated, looking around, knowing someone was out there. "Are we safe?"

"As safe as we can be. This is where the police come for coffee. There are always officers around."

Cora finally nodded. "Why exactly did you come today, again?"

Madigan smiled. "I told you. God said for me to." She held up a hand as Cora opened her mouth to protest. "Let me explain it to you, if I can. Silas and I were praying for you. He had a burden that you needed a place to live, where you would feel safe and not put your family at risk. We talked about it and he left it with me. I was praying for you after he left and Mrs. White's name came to mind. You know the rest."

"But I know Bill. He won't accept this."

"He will if he realizes it's a done deal and that you are making the move on your own. Silas was heading to talk with him today."

Before Madigan could say anything further, Cora interrupted. "Great. Now he'll know before I get a chance to talk with him."

"No, he won't. Silas will not say anything to him. He's like that. This is your life, your decision. Silas will support you in whatever decision you make, if he feels it's God's plan, and this time I know he does. He was heading to talk to Bill about something entirely different."

Cora sat, her eyes on the table top. "This is so different, Madigan. I'm not used to ministers like this."

"I know. Our old minister couldn't keep a confidence no matter how he tried, and he didn't try very hard. I felt bad when he would say something, not naming the person, but giving enough details we could always figure out who it was."

"That destroyed my trust in the church, you know." Cora twisted her mug on the table, not daring to look at Madigan, afraid of the condemnation she'd see there.

Madigan spoke softly. "It would, Cora, and I get that. So would Silas. If you need to talk to someone, please talk to me or talk to Silas. It goes not further unless you give us permission to share and it would only be with either Silas or myself, depending on who you talked with. Trust is too precious to destroy. And once it's lost, it's so hard to get back."

Cora raised her eyes to Madigan, movement near the road catching her eyes. She frowned, then sighed. "Just like I thought. I'm not safe here. One of those guys from yesterday is out there. Somehow they found me."

Madigan nodded. "It happened with Silas and I too. You don't know our story, do you?"

Cora shook her head. "Other than Bill saying you had an adventure."

"An adventure?" Madigan stared to laugh, causing Cora to stare at her, a frown on her face. "Seeing as I found a dead body in the church basement, we were run down in the parking lot, Silas lost his memory, we were kidnapped, assaulted, left for dead, and somewhere in there I lost my ability to speak. We still fell in love and married so quickly, far too quickly some thought. But he is the love of my life, Cora, and I think you'll find Bill is yours. He has that look in his eyes when he doesn't think anyone is watching him, that you're his one and only."

"But he was married, Madigan. How do I compete with her?"

"There's no competition, Cora. You are your own person. That's who he's in love with. Give him a chance, that's all he wants."

Madigan watched as Cora's attention kept going back outside. "Is someone out there, Cora?"

Cora nodded, sighing as she did so. "One of the men from yesterday. The tall one. I was so hoping they'd stay in jail forever."

Madigan gave a laugh and then looked around the cafe. "I see one of the officers from yesterday, Paul. He'll give us an escort back to your place."

"I can't ask that." Cora was horrified at the thought.

"You can't, but I can." Madigan was up and over talking to Paul before Cora could say anything.

Bill looked up as Silas walked towards him, handing him a cup of coffee. Bill took his with a quiet word of thanks, exhaustion rippling through his body. He hadn't slept the night before, too worried about Cora, too angry that the fight had been brought literally to his door in such a manner.

"How are you doing, Bill?" Silas watched Bill closely, knowing how he himself had felt when he was under attack.

"Hanging on but barely, Silas." He sipped at his coffee, his mind not on what he was doing. "How do I keep Cora safe? They brought it right to us, both of us."

"That's because they're after both of you. Somehow, somewhere, your lives connected during that time frame. Have you gone back over it all again?"

Bill nodded. "I have. I've talked to Elizabeth's people, to Wesley, to our friends from then. No one can figure out how she knew Cora."

"I don't think that she did, but I think she knew Lock or had seen him."

Bill paused, setting his cup on the railing. "How?"

"One of her classes, maybe. Was she in any of the college clubs?" Silas stared towards the back of the yard, not seeing the gardens Madigan had been working on rejuvenating.

Bill shook his head. "None. Other than what we were involved with at church. We spent most of our time together before we were married, and I don't remember her saying anything."

"Then, tell me. Did she go on any trips that you didn't?"

Bill's head shot around at that, and then his eyes slid closed. "She did. During our last semester of our junior year. It was a field trip to a rock formation that her geology prof took them too. She said there were other colleges there that day."

"Then, find out if Cora was there then too. I think that's your connection."

"Why didn't I think of it before?"

"Probably because you have buried a lot to do with Elizabeth's dying the way she did. You didn't get closure, haven't had closure, and need it."

Bill nodded, knowing his friend and pastor was right. "I need to have closure on this, Silas. We both do. But the thing is, even if we do, I don't know if Cora will stick around."

Silas just smiled. "I think she will. I've seen how she's been looking at you. You're her friend, Bill, and she's glad you're back in her life." He pulled out a chair at the table and pointed to another one. "Now, let's see if we can make some plans to catch these people." He paused as his phone chimed, then groaned. "She didn't, did she?"

"Madigan?"

"No, Cora. Madigan said she sent in a travelogue highlighting Elmton."

Bill sat, mulling over the possibilities and dangers of Cora doing just that, then shook his head. "I figured she'd do something like this. She's gone on the offensive. You don't stand in her way when she does that."

Andrew looked up as Lily appeared at his door, knocking softly, before he waved her in, watching as she shut the door behind her.

"What do you have, Lily?"

"That guy really documented everything." She shook her head. "He was on the prowl for young women he could take advantage of, usually to test a new drug on, without their knowing it. He names Elizabeth as one he was watching. He had seen her when she was on a class trip. I don't know yet how he managed to get on that trip when he wasn't even registered in a college that went there."

"I see. What about Cora?"

"He was stalking her for years, since high school from what we can gather. There's still a lot to work through. He does give names and I have a couple of detectives working that right now. Everyone wants this over for Bill and are working on their own time. I can't stop them."

Andrew gave a small smile, knowing that's what had been happening. "I didn't think we could. Just make sure they get down time. With Bill off, we need them on other cases as well. Nothing gets shoved to the side unless I say it does. Make sure they know that."

"They do, Andrew." Lily sat back, her eyes on her notes, not quite sure how to ask what she needed to ask.

"What do you need to know, Lily?"

She raised her eyes, seeing the look in Andrew's eyes, that he knew what she wanted to ask. "How serious is Bill about Cora?"

Andrew shrugged. "I have no idea. He's waiting on God for that one, Lily. Only God knows the plans He has for those two."

Lily nodded as she rose. "Do I need to talk to Bill about this?"

Andrew shook his head. "Not yet. Do more digging first."

Chapter 15

*H*earing someone clear their throat at the door of her new place, Cora peeked out from the kitchen and sighed. Bill had found her and she just knew she was in for a lecture.

She had been able to move all her belongings in that day and was working to get settled.

Bill stood and watched closely as Cora slowly made her way towards him, an uncertain look on her face. He gave a half-smile, which she frowned at.

"Bill? How did you find me?"

"Your Mom. She said you packed up and moved out. She understands but wishes you hadn't."

She sighed as she leaned against the wall. "I know she does, but I needed to."

Bill leaned against the door, legs crossed, hands jammed into his jacket pocket, staring back out the door. "I know you did. But can we talk about something else?"

She nodded, turning back to the kitchen. "Come on back. Have you had your dinner yet?"

"I'm not hungry, but eat if you want to." He slid the coffee carafe off the hot plate and filled their mugs, doctoring Cora's the way she liked before he slid it onto the table. He sat beside her, his head bowed in prayer, trying to gather the words he needed, to express to her what he had to say.

"Spit it out, Bill. You've never had a problem talking to me before."

He studied her face, then reached for her hands. "I know I haven't, but this is so hard." He bit at his lower lip. "I talked to Silas today. He asked how you and Elizabeth would have connected while at school. During your junior year, did you go on a trip to a rock formation an hour or so from Oak City?" When she nodded, her eyes watchful but questioning him, he continued, "Elizabeth did too. I think that's how you two were connected, that Lock saw you both and went from there."

She nodded. "I've already figured it was something like that, but never made the connection. I know there were a lot of colleges there that day. Do we know how he picked the ladies he wanted to stalk?"

Bill shook his head. "Lily says she working on that very thing, working through the journals. She and Andrew have talked, but are keeping me out of the loop, as well they should." He looked around the kitchen, standing to go into the living room and look around. "Are you satisfied with this place?"

"I am." She called back, her back to the kitchen door as she rinsed her dishes, not seeing the speculative look Bill shot her. "Why?"

"I just want you to be safe, Cora. I couldn't take losing another lady I love."

She spun at his words, her soapy hands held in the air, shock on her face, shaking her head as she took in what he said. "I'm too dangerous for you to get close to, Bill. You know that."

He approached her, ducking down so he could see into her face. "I know that the lady I love is in danger and I want to keep her as safe as I can. Does that bother you?"

She nodded. "It does. I mean, it shouldn't. You can't love me." She stammered to a stop, her eyes looking everywhere but at him.

He shook his head as he smiled, his hands reaching for hers. "We're both in danger right now, Cora, so it really doesn't matter does it? I don't know your feelings for me. I sense what they are but you will tell me when and if the time is ever right."

She nodded, then moved away. "Where do you think they'll strike next, Bill? They don't seem to have much of a plan, do they? Striking at various times and venues?"

Bill frowned, then nodded. "You're right. There really isn't a plan there, unless that's their plan."

She spun. "What do you mean?"

"Exactly that. They may want us to think that they don't have a plan, but they really do. Random attacks. That makes it difficult to plan or protect ourselves because we don't know when they will strike again." He walked towards her and hugged her. "I think you've just hit on the bigger picture, Cora."

She shook her head. "I'm not following you."

"They want us disoriented and looking around for them at all times. That keeps us on edge. When someone is on edge, that's when they make mistakes." He spun, searching for something.

"What are you looking for now, Bill?"

"A pen and paper. I need to make a plan."

Cora shook her head as she headed for her office. "In here. I've set the sun room up as my office."

Bill stood, looking around. "I like this. I need one of these rooms at my home. You can design it for me, Cora."

She shook her head again as she thrust pen and paper at him. "Now, will you let me in on what you're planning?"

"As soon as I figure out what it is I am planning." He grinned at her, then dropped to the floor, paper in front of him, pen poised over it. "Let's see. Going back to the rock formation and moving forward. Rock formation. Hiking trail. Your rock formation where you fell and injured your knee. Outdoors. River where they tossed us over the railing. What else?"

She sat beside him, shoulder to shoulder, and thought about what he was detailing. "It looks as if they are seeking outdoor venues where there may or may not be a lot of people around, depending on what they are planning. If they are testing a new drug, they wouldn't want many onlookers. If they are wanting to harm us, then the more people around, the easier it is for them to hit and run and get lost in the crowd. They'd be gone before anyone saw them." She paused. "In outdoor venues like they've been using, you don't get the security cameras you do in more settled, urban, shopping areas."

Bill paused in jotting down notes. "I think you're right, Cora darlin'. That's exactly why they're doing what they can. Trying to grab you after they set the fire was a crime of opportunity I think. You weren't supposed to walk away. The fire chief said it was set to burn only the garage and was likely a warning of some kind."

She stared at his use of an endearment, thinking he didn't mean it until he looked up, grinned and winked at her. She shook her head. God, where is Bill going with this? Doesn't he understand I'm not sure if or when I'll be ready for anything? But I guess You know best.

She looked down at the papers, then reached for more and took the pen from Bill's hand, writing her own name on one page, Elizabeth's on another and Lock on the third. Bill frowned as she did so, until she looked up, determination on her face.

Two hours later, she sat back, satisfaction on her face. She had listed every town, site, place she could think of that she had visited over the last two years. Bill had worked on Elizabeth's. She had listed what she had known of Lock's, but frowned as she looked at it.

"I think we need to give a copy of this to Lily. She has his journals and has the names of where he would have gone. That is, if we can trust what he's written."

"Why would you say that?" Bill studied her notes and then her face.

"Because he seemed to lie about everything else." She laid her cheek on her upraised knees, her eyes on him. "I'm finding I didn't really know the man I thought I loved. He was a very good liar, able to cover his tracks so well. Why didn't I see that, Bill?"

Bill shrugged. "I don't have an answer for that, Cora. I'm not sure we will ever know exactly what he was up to, not unless he confided in someone who eventually talks to us." He rose, gathering up their papers. "I'll need to make copies of these."

Cora pointed to her printer. "Use that. It has a copy function. Make one for yourself as well, so we can work on it when we're not together."

Bill nodded, his eyes searching the room and then the windows. Cora watched him, before she smiled.

"You've gong into cop mode on me, Bill. Now stop. Take your papers and head home. It's late."

Bill hesitated, knowing she was right. "Call me if you need me? If anything seems odd or you're worried?"

"I will. Now go."

Lily studied the paperwork Bill had left for her the next morning, a crow of victory rising from her. Andrew stopped in her doorway, a puzzled look on his face.

"Lily?"

She looked up, a grin on her face. "Bill and Cora have been busy. Bill said it was Cora's idea. They have listed every place, site, event they can think of for Cora, Elizabeth and Lock. All I need to do is go back through the journals and see what I can find. Then we'll set up a data entry program to link the three and see where they've crossed paths."

Andrew grinned back at her. "You can tell Bill not to come to work, but he'll still work. Sounds as if those two were busy. Keep me updated." He looked behind him, then entered and closed the door. "Lily, I need you to stay close to the two of them, you and Sam, as close as you can. Things are setting up to break wide open. I can't put anyone new on them or it will look suspicious to whoever is watching them. Sam's a friend from years ago. Bill's a colleague."

Lily looked at him and then down at her work and sighed. "How be Sam and I clone ourselves? Would that work?"

Andrew started to laugh. "It would, if we could. Do your best about that. I don't want it public knowledge that's what we're doing. And I know Bill will get suspicious if you hang around him too much."

Lily nodded. "We'll do what we can, Andrew. For now, this will keep me busy."

A week later, Cora stood, her eyes searching the church for Bill. He had asked her to come with him to the worship team practice and then had had to leave her on her own. She didn't see him and turned from the sanctuary, searching through the basement and then heading back for the stairs when the lights went out. She froze, not sure where the stairs were in her panic. She heard steps approaching her and turned, hoping it was Bill.

Instead she felt her arms caught in a tight grip as she was forced towards the stairs. Struggling, she broke free and ran, stumbling against the stairs as she was tackled. A scream broke from her throat as she was pulled to her feet and shoved up the stairs. She could hear running feet as she was pulled faster towards the exit. She struggled again, getting an arm free and hitting at the man holding her. He cursed at her as her hand hit his eye and his hold loosened. Free, she ran from him, searching for a place to hide. She didn't see the men running her direction, until she was caught and held tight in Bill's arm, then turned from the commotion and taken to a seat in Silas' office. Bill sat her down, then stood and stared, thoughts racing through his mind, before he turned and walked out the door, closing it behind him. Josiah and Adam nodded at him as they took up positions in front of it.

Bill walked towards the man Sam was holding on to. He frowned. The man looked familiar but he couldn't place him. Bill had a few words of quiet conversation with Sam before he turned to the man, who remained silent as both Bill and Sam questioned him.

Bill watched as Sam walked the man out to the patrol car, knowing Cora would have to give yet one more statement. When does it end, Lord? When will she be safe once more? She can't take much more, and frankly, neither can I where she's concerned.

Silas stopped beside him, his eyes concerned. "How's Cora?"

"In shock. Wanting this over. How do we go on, Silas? How do we keep her safe?"

Silas prayed for the right answers, knowing he didn't have them himself. "I'm not sure, Bill. What does your heart say?"

Bill snorted. "You know exactly what it says. What yours said about Madigan."

"Then I guess you have a conversation to have with Cora. If Madi or I can help in any way, let me know." He looked up towards the platform. "I guess this means practice is over. We really don't need to finish tonight. Let's gather everyone for prayer before we go. If you and Cora want to stay in the office and talk, feel free to. I'll come find you when we're done." His hand rested briefly on Bill's shoulder before he walked away, Bill's quiet thanks ringing in his ears.

Bill cracked the door open to the office and then stood, his eyes on Cora, his heart breaking at the fear he saw in her face as she looked up. He walked over and crouched down in front of her, his hands reaching for hers. She would have none of that, reaching to hug him instead. He held her for a few minutes, before he rose and scooped her into his arms, sitting back down in her chair.

"What are we to do, Cora? How do I keep you safe?"

She shrugged, her hair brushing against his chin. "I don't know, Bill. They seem to find me everywhere I go, not matter the place." She leaned back. "How do we both stay safe? It could have easily been you."

He shook his head. "No. They want you. They seem to think you have something they want." His arms tightened around her. "Cora, we need to talk. You know I love you. I just can't read what you're feeling."

She sighed, laying her head on his shoulder. "I love you too, Bill. It's just been so sudden. Almost too sudden."

"Not really. God is using our friendship from the past to build our future." He leaned back once more, a hand tracing her cheek. "We need to make a decision. Where do we go from here? I want you in my life. I want to grow old with you, for as many years as God grants us."

She nodded, her eyes on him. "So, is that a proposal or what?"

He broke out in laughter, hugging her tight before he kissed her. He moved away, then back for another kiss, relishing the love he felt from her.

Silas stood in the doorway, a delighted grin on his face. "Is this what I think it is?"

"Go away, Silas. Let me kiss my lady in peace."

Silas gave a shout of laughter. "Only for a few minutes. Then if you two want to talk to me, I'll be in the sanctuary. The rest are packing up to go home." He walked away, a delighted grin on his face. He needed to find his own wife and steal some kisses from her.

Cora smacked Bill on the arm, then shoved to her feet. "What did you just do, Bill?"

"Cora, darlin', I just staked my claim on you. Silas and Madigan have already suspected it." He reached for her hands. "How long a courtship should we have?"

She just shook her head. "Let's pray over this for a few days, Bill. It's so new for me."

"That we can do. But not too long, okay?"

Andrew stared at Bill as he stood in Andrew's living room the next day. "You did what?"

"I asked Cora to marry me." Bill paced, his mind not on the danger but on the woman he loved.

Andrew sighed. This was so not Bill, he thought. "And what did she say?"

"She's praying about it." Bill spun. "How's the investigation going?"

Andrew shook his head. "It's going. What you and Cora did with those lists is helping immensely. Lily and her team are working on a program to compare the lists. She's hoping for some results today." Andrew shook his head again. "You just had to do what the others did, didn't you?"

Bill grinned again as he moved towards the door. "I just wanted to give you a head's up. Let me know if you need us for anything. I'm off to find my lady."

Phoebe stood beside Andrew as he watched the door close, then reached to hug him. "He's smitten, isn't he?"

Andrew laughed as he kissed his wife. "About as much as I am with you. I think we'll have a wedding in a couple of weeks. I can't see them waiting long."

Phoebe joined in his laughter. "Nor can I. Now about that trip you were talking about? When were you thinking?"

Chapter 16

$\mathcal{A}$ week later, Cora stood, her hand resting on her father's arm as they stood at the back of the church. She was dressed in her mother's wedding dress, a simple gown of white satin and lace, her hair caught back with a gold clip of her grandmother's.

Her father watched her face. "You're sure, Cora?"

"Absolutely, Dad. It's different this time. I have no doubts."

"Then, let's go find your fellow." He dropped a kiss on her cheek. "Your mother and I like Bill awfully well. He's been good to you through the years."

She looked up, tears swimming in her eyes. "You couldn't say that about Lock. I'm glad you can about Bill."

Bill turned as Cora approached him, taken aback by her beauty. Lord, make me worthy of her. Guide us in our new lives.

The church was full of their family and friends, fellow officers of Bill's as well. The officers kept their eyes open, looking for anyone who didn't belong. The two men standing across the street had no chance of making it into the church, staring around at the number of officers there, before walking away. They would have to try another day and that day, they would be successful in nabbing those two.

A week later, Cora wandered through Bill's home, now her home. She had not expected to fall in love with her long-time friend, but she could see God's hand at work. She turned as she felt Bill's arms around her.

"Happy, darlin'?"

"I am, Bill. And you?"

He nodded. "I am. Just wish we could catch the guys after you." He sighed. "I'm back to work on Monday and I don't want to leave you. I'll worry about you the whole time I'm gone."

"Just as I'll worry about you. It's okay. I have some work to do on videos the boss wants to revisit. I need to plan another trip somewhere to get more pictures. Is there still the quarry near Riverville?"

"There is. We can head there on the weekend if you like."

She nodded. "That would be good. I'd like to showcase the area around here. I have no desire to travel anymore." She sighed. "I guess I'm going to have to tell my boss that."

"In time, Cora. Don't rush into it." He stepped back, his hand reaching for hers. "Let's go to Ev's for dinner."

She shook her head. "Too open and too many people will question. Can we go out of town?"

"That we can. Let me see what I can come up with." He groaned as his phone chimed. "This is not a good time. It's Andrew." He sighed. "I guess I have to answer it, do I?"

Cora started to laugh. "No, you don't but you might want to. Who knows what he wants."

"Andrew? You're interrupting a very important discussion here about where we head for dinner." Bill grinned as Cora shook her head at him.

"Am I? Sorry about that." Andrew sounded distracted. "Listen. You're back to work on Monday, right? Good. Lily's still working full time on your case. I have some others I need to get you up to speed on but Monday will work for that. Can you and

Cora join Phoebe and I on Sunday for dinner?"

"I'll ask Cora, but we did sort of have plans."

"That's fine, Bill. Another day will work." Andrew's voice faded away. "Listen. Something's come up. I need to run. Stay safe, you two."

Bill frowned as he pocketed his phone. "That was strange. It didn't sound like Andrew at all."

"Check the number and see if it was his. Or else call him back." Cora watched as Bill pulled his phone back out, scrolling through the numbers.

"It wasn't a number I recognize him calling from. And it really didn't sound like him." He dialed Andrew's number, getting his voice mail and leaving a message for him to call. "I can't do much more than that."

The men standing across the street watched as Bill and Cora drove away, before they crossed to Bill's house. They searched for an entry, finding none, but noting the security system he had in place. They could work around that, they thought. Plans were falling into place and soon, Bill and Cora would be in their hands.

Three weeks later, Bill was back hard at work, the cases he was assigned piling up. He sighed as he looked at the pile. He needed to get home early tonight and wasn't sure if he could make it. He looked up as Lily stopped at his desk.

"Bill? Why are you still here?"

He shrugged. "I was just finishing up a report and time got away from me. I'm out of here soon." He stared at the pen he was rolling in his fingers. "I know you can't say much, Lily, but how close to solving our case have you come?"

"We're getting there, Bill. Ted and I are heading out tomorrow to do some more interviews. You'll be in early, right?"

He nodded. "I will be. That's what we agreed I'd do." He rose, grabbing for his suit jacket. "I'll pick up my work tomorrow. It appears I'm stuck in the office for the duration."

She laughed as she walked out with him. "Say hi to Cora for me."

The next morning, Andrew looked up from the paperwork he was immersed in to see Lily frantically pacing towards his office, her phone to her ear.

"Have you see Bill?" Her words brought him to his feet.

"No. I haven't. I've been in my office since I got in. Why?"

"He was supposed to be here at 7, to cover early calls and didn't show up. Dispatch called me at 8 when they couldn't raise him."

Andrew's heart sank. "Have a patrol officer go by his house. I'm heading that way. Lily?"

She turned from where she was almost running to the parking lot. "I'm going too. Bill's in trouble, Andrew. I can just feel it."

Andrew threw open his car door and ran for Bill's front door, meeting the patrol officer coming around from the back. "Anything?"

Tad, the officer, shook his head. "The security system line has been cut. I was just about to go in."

Andrew reached for the door knob, finding it turned easily under his hand. This was not Bill. If he wasn't home, the door was locked. "His car?"

"Still in the garage, and I think it's likely Cora's car too. I haven't had a chance to run the plates yet. A small gray SUV."

"That's hers." Andrew drew his weapon and entered, searching each room, Tad following. Finally, he shoved his weapon back in the holder. "There's no sign of them."

"Andrew?" Tad pointed towards the living room. "I think they were taken against their will. There's some signs of a struggle there."

Andrew turned to where Tad had pointed, then froze. "On the wall. That's blood. But from which one?" He turned, hand on Tad's shoulder. "Outside now. I want an officer assigned to front and back doors. Not you. You'll be giving a statement as will I. Call for the techs, will you?"

Andrew walked down to his car, rubbing the back of his neck, concern coursing through him. Where were they? It didn't look good, he thought. Who had taken them and why? He looked up to see Lily standing in front of him, shock on her face.

"Andrew?" Her voice was hopeful.

"They're not there, Lily." He spun to stare at the house. "There are signs of a struggle and some blood. Whose, I have no idea." He looked around. "Is Ted here too?"

She nodded. "Over there by the garage."

"Okay. Here's what we're doing. You go get Tad's statement. Ted will take mine. We're have the techs come through. Officers have been assigned to the doors and to search the surrounding area. We need to find them, Lily, but I don't think we'll find them near here at all."

Lily hesitated, horror and fear on her face for a moment before she composed herself. "I will. Andrew? Do you think they're still alive?"

Andrew nodded. "I do. They'll keep them alive as long as they have hope of getting whatever it was that Lock left. And whatever it is he buried in those journals. Did you find anything at all?"

She shook her head. "Not yet. I have a cryptologist going over them right now, to see if he can find anything."

Andrew nodded. "There's one other thing we can try. Contact Emma or Jace at Tracker's in Riverville. She's good at what she does and has resources we don't. Fill her in on what we have. Let her know it's Bill, and she'll drop everything to work on it."

Lily stared at him, having heard of Tracker's. "Emma?"

"That's right. Emma and her husband, Abe, are good friends of ours. If we need to, he has a security team that we can pull in to help us."

Andrew stood near his car later, watching the activity surrounding Bill's house, the techs going in and out. His heart raised in prayer as he stood, uncertain as to what to do or where to go. Hearing his name called in a low voice, he turned and walked towards Silas.

"Andrew? Don't tell me!" Silas wore a look of concern and worry.

"Someone took them, Silas. Who or when, we're not sure. Bill was due in at 7 and never showed. The last anyone saw him was about 4:30 yesterday when Lily walked out with him."

Silas breathed a silent prayer even as he searched the area. "Are they hurt?"

"One of them is for sure. I saw blood on the wall in the entryway." He turned to watch the house once more.

"Madigan felt somewhat was up. That's why I'm here. I called and let her know to put out the prayer chain calls, asking for safety for our two. We don't need to know much more than that to pray for them."

"No, we don't, do we? I know God has them in the hollow of His hand, but I still want them here and safe." Andrew ran a hand through his hair. "Can I get you to talk to the others in the group? Call for a prayer time at our place tonight? I'm not sure if I'll get there but Phoebe will be. If you can't make it, ask Josiah to chair."

"That I can do. And both Madi and I will be there. Someone else can chair the meeting at the church tonight. You need me with you."

Andrew nodded, a somber look on his face. "I just wish we could have solved it before it got this far."

"God didn't mean for you to do that. If He had, it would have been solved. There's a reason He's allowing this, Andrew. Just keep that in mind."

Andrew groaned as his phone chimed once more and he pulled it out. "Wesley. Now how do I tell him? Wesley?"

"Andrew? Have you seen Bill? I need to talk to him asap and can't raise him. Not at work. Not on his cell." Wesley's tone was fraught with worry.

"That's the thing, Wesley. Both he and Cora are missing." He held the phone away from his ear as Wesley yelled. "I'm at his place right now. They're not here and there seems to have been a struggle of some kind."

"Were either one of them hurt, can you tell?"

"Not really. The techs will tell me more." Andrew slowly turned in a circle, feeling the eyes watching him, but not seeing anyone. "What about your wife and kids?"

"They're tucked away somewhere safe. They have been for a while now."

"That's good. Listen. Tell your captain what's up, but no one else, okay? I'm not sure who I can trust on your task force, given we know some are involved."

"I will. If I can, I'm heading your way this afternoon. It depends on where we are standing here."

Andrew tucked his phone away and turned in a circle once more before heading back towards the house and the lead tech who stood waiting for him. This was not how he

planned to spend his day. He had paperwork
he had to get to today. It looked as if he'd be
in the office for quite a while.

Chapter 17

*R*olling over to his back, Bill's hand dragged across his chest to cradle the soreness of his ribs, the other arm draped across his eyes. His body was sore and bruised, having taken beatings almost daily. He listened but could hear no sounds. He had no idea what day it was, how long they had been here, or even where they were, they had been moved every few days. He rolled back to his side, groaning slightly as he did, trying not to alert their guards. He raised his head, searching for Cora, seeing her curled up across the room from him, her head on her arm, her other arm wrapped around her in an attempt to keep warm.

He knew he couldn't get to her. Whoever had kidnapped them had made sure of that, with a chain fastened around his ankle. He knew Cora was fastened the same. Would today be the day it all ended, he wondered? He knew they couldn't go on much longer. Lord, save Cora, please. It doesn't matter much about me. Please keep my wife alive.

His head dropped back to the floor and his eyes closed, not quite asleep, not quite awake. His mind drifted back to that night they were taken.

Cora had been waiting for him that night when he walked through the door, eagerly coming into his arms for his hug and kiss. She had urged him to change into his jeans, sweatshirt and hiking boots, pointing to the cooler where she had packed their dinner. An impromptu picnic, he thought. Just what they both needed. She grabbed her favourite camera as they headed out, heading for a conservation area near them, one they had frequented as teens.

Heading home, they had stopped at their favourite ice cream shop, just like they used to. Cora had found some favourite music at home and they had cuddled up on the couch, Cora pulling a blanket over her as she snuggled up to him, their conversation quiet and not really about anything in particular. They had both nodded off, not realizing what horror lay ahead of them.

A small click had awakened him a couple of hours later, causing him to raise his head and listen. He carefully moved Cora away from him and went to stand, the small round end of a gun barrel jammed into his neck stopping him. He froze, not knowing who had managed to get into their home or even how. The security system hadn't gone off, he thought.

He heard a small sound from Cora as she was pulled to her feet and shoved towards the door. He lunged towards the man holding her and fell, the blow to his head temporarily stopping him. He was hauled to his feet, staggering as he tried to catch his balance. He wiped his hand across the side of his head, then reached the bloodied hand to the wall to keep upright. He too was shoved forward, arm held tight in a grip as he struggled to free himself and get to Cora.

He saw the panic and fright on her face as she was shoved into a vehicle, then he was pushed into another seat. He heard a small cry from her as she went limp. He rose, intent on reaching her when he felt a small prick on his neck. His vision faded as his body collapsed. Drugged was all he had time to think before the world went black.

Day after day, they were roused and questioned, the same questions repeated in various ways. Always the same, he thought, just different men asking them. How many men were there? He had lost track of the number. At first, there were not beatings. Then the slaps and blows started. Each day, the beatings got worse. He knew he wouldn't last much longer. He was always made to stand or sit with his back to Cora. He couldn't tell how much of a beating she took each day. He knew she had been. He had her low cries and whimpers, sounds that broke his heart and made him struggle to get to her, earning him more beatings. He had heard her begging them not to hurt him, to hurt her instead. She was adamant that she did not know what they were looking for, nor did he. She had nothing left of Lock's, she maintained.

He turned that final day they were held, staggering as he did so, the only thing holding him upright the hand on his arm. His blurry eyes sought for Cora, seeing her seated in a chair, her arms bound to it. He shook his head to clear his vision, regretting it as the three dozen drummers that had taken up residence there began their practice. He groaned, drawing Cora's eyes to him. She grimaced, her eyes red from crying, pain evident in them and on her face. But her love for him came through as she mouthed the words "I love you" to him.

Bill was shoved towards another room. The men didn't seem to care that he was a police officer they had assaulted. His hands were bound above his head and he tilted his head carefully to look up. There was no way he would ever be able to get free on his own. His head dropped as his heart grew heavy. Lord, why? Where's our help? Have You forgotten about us?

He heard the whimpers and sobs from Cora and tried to free his hands, unable to avoid the blows and slaps. His eyes closed as he heard a sharp cry from Cora and then the blackness took over. His head slumped forward even as his body sagged, the only thing holding him upright the bonds tying his wrists to the beam overhead.

Cora's heart stuttered in her chest as she recognized the voice of the man who stood behind her. Things became crystal clear to her. She now knew who had been after them, but would she live to talk to anyone? She doubted it. She had been praying for release, to be free and able to carry on her life with Bill. Today, she lost hope. Today, they broke her. Tears sparkled in her eyes, blinding her for a moment. Then clarity peeked through. She shuddered as she saw the syringe being laid on the table in front of her. She knew she faced the same fate as others, as Elizabeth likely had. She shook her head, unable to speak, at the questions hurled at her. Her head sank as she lost her will to fight, to continue to live. Her head was pulled back roughly, and curses rang through the room as the men realized that they could get no more answers from either of the couple.

Then, the guard from the door raced into the room, shouting that they needed to leave, that they had been found. The men scattered, leaving the debris and evidence behind them. Bill and Cora didn't see them leave, didn't hear the sounds of car doors slamming, of rapid footsteps running for the building, the doors being opened, and then footsteps pacing rapidly towards them as the building was searched.

Neither one of the young couple heard the cries of dismay and urgency as Cora was discovered, her bonds loosened, arms reaching to catch her as she slid forward in the chair, to gently lower her to the floor. They didn't hear further calls for assistance as Bill was found and loosened from his bonds. They didn't hear the commotion that ensued around them as paramedics rushed in to triage and then prepare them for transport. They didn't see Bill's fellow officers and friends watching as the stretchers were rushed from the building to the waiting ambulances, didn't hear the sirens as the vehicles sped from the building, full escort in place.

Andrew shifted as quietly as he could on the hard seat in the courtroom. He had been called to testify that day in a case that went back to when he had still been a lieutenant on the county force. His mind really wasn't on the proceedings now that his part was done, but he had been asked to wait until the noon recess just in case he was needed again. He sensed someone at his shoulder and looked up to see one of the court bailiffs bending over to speak with him, pointing back towards the door. He stood, making his way quietly from the room, the judge looking up with a frown and then a nod to the bailiff as he turned to follow Andrew.

Andrew's steps slowed as he approached Lily, who stood waiting for him, barely contained her anxiety.

"Lily? This had better be good. I was asked to stay until the noon recess." Andrew's voice was stern, but his eyes compassionate as he studied the young detective.

She nodded. "I understand. You know I wouldn't disturb you unless I had news. We think we've found the building. I'm setting up the response team to go in. You will want to be part of that, I know. And I've asked dispatch to set up road blocks around the area."

Andrew nodded even as he walked rapidly towards the doors. "Where?"

"The old Walters building, near the outskirts of town. Someone finally reported seeing vehicles going in and out of there for the last few days. They didn't want to get involved, they said."

Andrew snorted as he slid behind the wheel of his car and Lily shut the passenger door behind her. "Of course, they didn't. How sound is the tip?"

"Very. Tad went out and scouted around. There were about three or four vehicles, he said, a couple of high-end ones."

Andrew stood outside the building, his suit coat thrown carelessly in his car trunk, tightening his body armour over himself as he watched the ETF men and women prepare to enter. He would be right in there with them. There was no way he was staying out, not when his friends could be in there. He walked rapidly towards the ETF leader and spoke quietly with him.

He followed as the team searched the building, clearing room after room. He heard the dismayed cry as they found Cora, reaching to catch her as she was freed from her bonds, laying her gently on the floor, then stepping back as one of the women assessed her, turning to ask for the paramedics.

His head shot up as he heard Sam yelling for him, that he had found Bill. He ran, dust kicking up from under his feet, and slid to a halt, momentarily taken aback at the sight of Bill's slumped body, the only thing holding him up the bonds tying his hands above his head. He saw Sam frantically dragging a chair across the room even as he dug out a pocket knife before he was up on the chair, reaching for the rope. Andrew's arms went around his friend's limp body and he pulled it upwards to ease the ropes.

He staggered as Bill's right arm dropped as it was freed and his body sagged against his hold. He widened his stance and shifted Bill's body more upright, one hand going to hold Bill's left arm. Sam was off the chair once Bill's other arm was free, reaching for his legs to help carry him to the paramedics waiting near Cora. Sam knelt beside Bill, his knife cutting at the bonds that still encased his wrists, carefully setting them aside as he freed Bill. He knew the team would want them for evidence.

Andrew stood back, his eyes on his friends, as the paramedics worked to stabilize them, start the IVs and get them ready to transport. He caught Ezra's eyes, causing Ezra to stand from where he was working on Cora and walk towards him.

"Ezra?"

"They're alive, Andrew. I don't know how, given the beatings and abuse they've taken. How long was it?"

"Two weeks, sixteen days, something like that." Andrew's eyes didn't leave the couple, not seeing the speculative look and then the compassion that flooded Ezra's eyes.

When Ezra didn't speak, Andrew nodded, his gaze searching the room. "Anything else? I'll have you escorted to the hospital."

Ezra nodded to the table. "There's a full syringe there. We haven't touched it. It doesn't look as if it's been used, but we can't tell for sure. I'll have them run a full drug panel on them."

Andrew's eyes shot to the table and then he walked towards it, a frown on his face. "I hope they can test for this drug, but if it's one of the new ones that I suspect they were making, I doubt they'll be able to identify it." He spun as he heard his name and saw Lily motioning for him.

"Lily? What can you tell me?" Andrew watched her face, seeing concern but victory mixed on it.

"We have two of the men. They were stopped at a roadblock trying to get out of town. Ted heading downtown to talk to them, but he suspects they'll lawyer up. The other vehicles, we can see which way they went but they headed into town, so without a description or plate number, we can't do much. Tad, I think, got plate numbers and he'll work that."

"Good. Now, about this scene?"

"The techs have pretty much dropped whatever they were working on and all of them are headed this way."

Andrew turned and searched the area, feeling eyes watching from somewhere, but not seeing anyone. "Someone's still here, Lily. I can feel the eyes on us. Have the team spread out more and search deeper. I want these guys."

"We all do, Andrew. Are you heading to the hospital?"

He turned as he watched the ambulances pull away, full police escort in place. "I will shortly. I just want to make sure everything is in place here. I don't want us to miss anything. Not one thing."

Lily nodded, turning to search the area around. "How did we not know, Andrew? They've been in town the whole time, I suspect, and we never knew, never found them."

"If who I think is heading this, it's no wonder we didn't find them. He has deep pockets and lots of buildings."

Lily turned to search his face. "You know who it is?"

Andrew shook his head. "Just a suspicion. Nothing I could prove." He finally sighed, reaching for his car keys, staring down as them as he ran his fingers over them. "Stay here, Lily. Make sure everything's done by the book. I don't want anything missed. I don't want to get to court and have something thrown out because we rushed it, or didn't do what we should have."

He looked up, his eyes shuttered, even as he breathed out a prayer for his friends. He prayed they hadn't been too late. He had seen the looks on the paramedics' faces even as they tried to hide them. They didn't hold out much hope for the two.

He sighed as he reached for his phone. He needed someone to go find Cora's parents. He dreaded the call he had to make to Wesley, but he would be the one, not one of the officers. He first called the Brodies, letting them know an officer was on his way to their place, that they had found Cora and Bill, but he didn't know how serious their condition was.

He paused, his eyes on his phone, as he leaned back against the trunk of his car, his eyes raising as he heard talk around him. He turned, his fingers finding Wesley's number.

"Andrew? Tell me you have news?" Wesley's voice echoed over the phone. Andrew could tell he was on the road.

"Wesley! Where are you?"

"About 20 minutes out. Why?"

"Head for the hospital. I'll meet you there."

There was silence on the phone. Andrew could hear the ragged breath Wesley drew in and knew he was trying to control his emotions, but without much success.

His voice thick, Wesley spoke. "He's alive?"

"He is, Wesley. I don't know how, but he is. They took him in about thirty minutes ago."

"Thank you, Andrew. You and your officers." There was silence again. "Cora?"

"She's there as well. The thing is, Wesley, they're in rough shape."

"I can only imagine how bad. I'll meet you there. I need to call my family."

"Do that."

Andrew slid his phone into his pocket, taking one last look around, confident that the scene was in good hands before he positioned himself behind his wheel and then bowed his head. Tears came, he couldn't stop them, as he prayed for the lives of his friends.

Chapter 18

$\mathcal{A}$ndrew shoved himself away from the wall in the Emergency Department waiting room he had been leaning against. He knew Phoebe was around here somewhere. She had met him as he arrived, spent some time with him, and then mingled with the officers and their families as they arrived. He thought she was likely in the chapel, where their friends had gathered. He could feel the adrenalin leaving his body, the fatigue and weariness setting in. He looked up as a cup of coffee appeared in his vision. Silas stood there, a concerned look on his face.

"Come on, Andrew. Outside. Walk with me. You've been standing here for four hours. You need to take a break. If you don't, your people won't."

Andrew searched the room, knowing that Silas was right. "Okay, just for a bit. When did you get here?"

"Right before you, I think. I've been spending time with Cora's people and then

Wesley. They're back with them now, I think."

Andrew dropped down at the staff picnic table, his head dropping to his folded arms. He sighed once more, trying to find the strength to go on.

Silas' hand rested on his shoulder as he prayed for his friends. He wiped at his eyes. He could only imagine how Andrew was feeling. It was more than an officer involved. Bill was a close friend and Cora was becoming that with Phoebe.

Andrew looked up, wiping at his face, unashamed of the tears. "Thank you, Silas."

"You're welcome, Andrew. Have you heard anything on their condition?"

Andrew shook his head. "Not really. I was going to go back soon, just for an update." He looked up at a noise and groaned. "Of course. The media is here, circling like vultures."

Silas gave a small grin. "Let your PR people deal with them for now. You need to be inside for your people. But you need your own strength to be replenished. Drink your coffee."

"Yes, mother."

Silas grinned at him, then stood. "Come on, my friend. Let's get you back inside before they see you."

Andrew headed for the exam rooms once back inside, watching as Cora's parents stood in the hallway, her father's arm around his wife. He looked up as Andrew approached, apprehension on his face.

"Mr. Brodie?"

"Andrew. Thank you for finding them." He nodded at the room. "They've taken her to do some X-Rays or a CT scan or something they said. The doctor wasn't happy with what he was feeling on her arm or abdomen."

Her mother looked up and then reached to hug Andrew. "Thank you."

Andrew stood with them for a while, them moved past them to where he knew he would find Bill. Wesley looked up as Andrew cracked open the door and walked into the room, his steps quiet.

"Wesley?"

Wesley walked towards him, shooting glances back over his shoulder. "Andrew. Thank you."

Andrew nodded. "How is he?"

"Battered. Bruised. He has some bleeding somewhere in the abdomen, but they're not rushing him to surgery. They're monitoring it for now but there's always the chance he'll end up in surgery. They want to run some more tests." He turned to look back at his brother. "They've run a drug panel as well. They found evidence of a sedative in his blood and they think both Bill and Cora have been sedated quite a bit." Wesley had to stop speaking, the emotions too much.

"No other drugs?" Andrew's thoughts turned to the syringe Ezra had found.

"No, not that they can tell. Why?"

"There was a loaded string found in the room where Cora was. We don't think it had been used yet. The lab running it to see what they can find out."

Andrew walked forward to stand at the end of the bed, his hands jammed into his pockets, his eyes on his friend. "He hasn't been awake at all?"

"No. They don't expect him to be. They want to sedate him, to give him time to heal, but Bill has written into his medical papers that he gets no sedation in a case like this. Absolutely none. That ties their hands." Wesley shot a look at the door. "How's

Cora? I haven't had a chance to talk to her parents."

"I haven't heard much about her. They were still doing tests, her parents said." Andrew paused, his eyes on Wesley. "I have to head back down town, to see where the investigation lies. I'll be back." He hesitated before he walked away. "There will be officers on their doors at all times. So many are volunteering we're having to draw names."

Wesley gave a tired smile. "That's about what I thought you'd say. When they go home, we'll need to look at some kind of security, if you haven't got them all by then."

"We'll address that when the time comes." Andrew looked back at Bill, not seeing any movement from him. "They'll be here for a few days, so we have time to work on a plan."

"And I can guarantee you Bill won't like it or want to go along with it."

Andrew gave a small laugh, knowing his friend well. "No, I don't think he will want to, but he will because of Cora."

Three days later, Bill groaned as he moved in the bed, feeling like every part of his body was sore. He cracked open his eyes, as much as he could for the swelling and looked around, a small frown on his face. He heard movement and jerked, the pain coursing through his body.

"Take it easy, Bill. Here, have some water. Your mouth and throat must be so dry." The lady's voice sounded familiar and he squinted at her. Wesley's wife. Anna.

"Thank you." He managed to get out the words. "Cora?"

"She's in the room across the hall. You're safe." She reached for the call button. "Your nurse wanted to know when you woke."

Bill's hand stopped her, and he stared at the splints on two fingers. "Wait. How is Cora?"

"She's sleeping, Bill. She's been awake today, her parents said."

"I want to see her." Bill tried to sit up, pushing at the blankets, falling back against the mattress, pain coursing through him.

"Not right now. Right now, you need to stay here."

Bill finally nodded, knowing he didn't have the strength to rise and go and find Cora.

His eyes slid shut and he slept. Wesley stood, leaning against the closed hospital door, his eyes on his brother before he walked forward and wrapped his wife in his arms, comforting her as best he could.

"He wanted to go to Cora, Wesley."

"I know he did. I'd have wanted to do the same." He turned as Andrew shoved the door open and entered, his eyes concerned.

"Wesley?"

"He was awake, Andrew. Tell me this is over."

Andrew shook his head, watching Bill closely, seeing the cuts and bruises on his face, the bandage marking the spot he had been struck so hard on that first night, that had kept opening up under his beatings, the bandages wrapped around his wrists where the rope had abraded them. "We're still looking for the top guys. We have an idea who they are but don't have confirmation on that yet."

Four days later, Bill sank gratefully down onto his couch, his eyes on Cora as she moved carefully towards her favourite chair. He sighed. How would they look after one another, Lord? I don't think we can. He took the mug Phoebe handed him before she turned to Cora.

Cora shook her head at whatever it was Phoebe had asked her. Bill hadn't managed to hear what it was, Phoebe's voice was that low. Cora raised her eyes to Bill, a look in them he couldn't read, before she laid her head back and closed them, drifting off to sleep. Bill knew she was hurting, not just physically. The emotional and mental torture she had undergone had been intense. He prayed for her healing in all ways.

Phoebe stood for a moment watching her friend before she turned to Bill, sitting on the coffee table in front of him.

"What can I get you, Bill?"

"Nothing right now, Phoebe. You need to get home."

"I will. I just want to make sure you two are okay. Your friends have sent in soup and stuff for sandwiches, soft foods, whatever it is you two feel like. Let us know what we can do for you. Please!"

Bill nodded, and regretted it right away. The drummers had decreased in number but were still there. He grimaced, a hand going to his temple. "We'll be okay, Phoebe. You need to get home. Make Andrew quit early today. If you don't, he won't."

"No one is quitting early right now, Bill. They're working as many hours as they can to find these people."

"And they will eventually, but it won't help if they get sick or injured because they're too tired to watch out for themselves."

"I'll make sure they know your sentiments." Phoebe rose, her gaze shifting between the two. "Call one of us, no matter what time of day or night? Okay?"

"We will." His eyes drifted shut as he heard the door close behind her. He cracked them open for a moment to watch Cora before he rose, gathering her into his arms and carrying her to the bedroom. He gently laid her on the bed and found a blanket to cover them both as he laid down beside her, his arm tight around her. He had almost lost her and didn't like that feeling.

Chapter 19

 *L*ate afternoon, Cora finally stirred, her senses warning her she was at home. She felt the heaviness of an arm over her and had momentary panic until she turned her head and saw Bill sound asleep beside her, cradling her to his body. She lay, studying his face, thankful he was still alive and with her. She prayed for complete healing for him, knowing she wouldn't want to go on if he wasn't with her.

She slipped away from the bed, heading for the kitchen, needing to find something to eat. She frowned at the remembered food in the hospital. No, she had not enjoyed it at all. Opening the fridge, she stood, her eyes full of wonder at the assortment of food there. Hearing a sound behind her, she spun, her hand to her chest. Tad stood there, an apologetic look on his face.

"I'm sorry, Cora. I thought you heard me come in the door."

"I think I did, but I'm not sure what all I'm hearing right now." She turned back to the fridge. "We have plenty of food. What would you like?"

He reached for the fridge door, startling her once more. "How be you sit and I'll get you something? You're not quite steady on your feet yet, are you?" He grinned as she shook her head.

"No, I'm not. A cup of tea would be nice." She moved away from him towards the cupboard, stopping to brace herself for a moment, finding his hand on her arm guiding her to a chair.

"Tell me where to find everything and I'll take care of it." His eyes raised as he saw Bill hesitating in the doorway. "Bill, you'll want coffee?"

Bill shook his head. "No, just some juice. Has Andrew been around?"

"He said he'd be by this evening. He has some news, I think. He wanted to talk to you both." Tad glanced at the clock. "He called me about two hours ago, said not to disturb either one of you as you were sleeping."

Bill nodded as he slid back a chair beside Cora, reaching for her hand as he sat, bringing it to his lips to kiss it. She watched him, a softening of her eyes telling him she loved him, but shaking her head at him in the same instance.

Tad finally walked away, heading for outside and the officer who had arrived to take over for him. He glanced back at the two, a frown in place. Something was off somewhere, and he didn't know where or what.

Later, Bill and Cora both looked up from where they still sat at the table, a frown on each of their faces at the steps coming towards. Bill rose, then froze as he saw Andrew shoved towards him, his hands cuffed behind him, blood dripping from a cut on his cheek. Cora gave a small scream, unable to help herself, before her hands covered her mouth.

Bill reached for Andrew but was knocked backwards by the man who had shoved Andrew towards them. Andrew lost his balance and fell heavily, his head hitting the hardwood floor, before he lay still. Bill backed towards Cora, his hand reaching for hers.

Cora's eyes were fixed on the man who then appeared in the doorway, her gasp alerting Bill. He frowned at the man. Why was he here? Cora's hand tightened on his, almost to the point that her grip crushed his hand. He moved in front of her, defying the man who had shoved him to come at him again.

"He's the one, Bill." Cora's whisper caught his ear and he nodded.

"Well, Cora. We meet again. This time, you don't get to walk away." The heavyset man walked towards her.

"I don't think so, Mr. Walters. Your time of ruining lives is over." Cora peeked around Bill. "Showing up here today? You've just signed the warrant for your arrest."

Bill stared at the man standing in front of them. Leo Walters was a popular principal at the local high school, had been there when he and Cora were in high school. How did he get mixed up in all this?

"I don't think so. No one will be left alive to say anything." He directed a kick at Andrew's leg. "No one saw us come in. So, don't get your hopes up?"

"Why?" Cora's voice broke through the silence that had descended.

"Money. Control. Status." Walters grinned at her. "Take your pick. Now, you."

He pointed at Cora. "You weren't supposed to survive last year. How you did, I really don't know. Lock was supposed to find what you had and then turn it over to us."

"I had nothing." Cora's voice had a bite, her anger barely controlled. Lord, she prayed, let this end now. Let Bill's friends come and find us before he kills us, and that he plans to do, I know. We won't leave here alive if no one shows up.

"I think you do. Lock said he gave it to you. Only, he didn't tell us what it was or when he gave it to you. Our searches didn't find it. You refused to talk, lying through your teeth that you never had anything of his that raised your suspicions."

"I have nothing left of his. Anything personal, I either gave away or dumped in the garbage months ago."

"You were in his locker."

Bill spoke up. "Just personal journals there. Nothing that named anyone or anything."

Walters was getting agitated, starting to pace, his hands tightening into fists. Bill watched closely, keeping an eye on the man with him. He dropped a glance at Andrew, who still lay quiet, eyes closed. Bill couldn't tell if he was unconscious or just pretending.

Bill heard a faint click of a lock and his eyes narrowed. It was the front door. It had to be someone on their side, he thought. Tad was supposed to have gone home an hour ago and left Terry out there. But who knows what had happened in the last hour. Somehow these two had gotten the drop on Andrew, and that was hard to do.

Cora's head tilted as she studied her former principal. Things clicked into place from years ago. She knew now who had been the one behind the attacks on her friends who stood up to those selling or using drugs.

"It was you all along, wasn't it? You're the brains behind the new drugs that went through the school. What did you give Elizabeth?"

Bill froze as she said that, his eyes hardening as he stared at Walters.

Walters laughed. "Nothing. That's the thing. We didn't give her a thing. She saw us and ran. They say fear can kill. I guess they are right."

Bill's hand clenched in anger. "Somehow, I don't think that's the truth. They found a needle mark on her arm,

Walters. So, yeah, you did give her something."

Walters stopped pacing, his eyes on Bill in disbelief. "No, she was given nothing."

Bill shook his head. "She was. Lock was there. We have evidence that she was drugged and that drug killed her."

Walters paced once more, his pace quickening in his agitation. "No. That can't be. They weren't supposed to try it out on anyone yet."

"Well, guess what?" Cora's voice lashed out at him. "They did. She's not the only one they did that to."

Walters spun, his eyes on Cora as she spoke, his henchman standing to the side, watching as well. Bill caught a hint of movement behind the men but kept his eyes on the two in front of him, his hand reaching once more for Cora's.

"So, is that your confession then? You dreamed up the drugs, had them manufactured and then distributed through here?"

Walters gave a laugh of triumph. "Sure, I'll confess. You've figured it out, not that it will do you any good. You won't live to tell anyone. None of you will." He gestured with his hand and his man pulled out the syringes they had prepared.

Bill's face whitened as he moved Cora back behind him and forced her back into the room more. He knew they were getting near the back door. He prayed he could reach it and get her out before they came at them with the drugs. He stopped as a gun appeared in the man's hand, pointed at Cora.

Cora's hand wrapped around Bill's wrist, her hand clenched tight in his. He felt her lean on him, her head against his back. He knew she was praying, just as he was. Would they make it out of this? Lord, please. Help us. We're stuck here, not able to get away. Andrew's hurt and no help to us.

"Step away from her, Buckley. You get to see this wife die."

Bill refused to move, his stance defiant, not giving an inch as Walters motioned at him. Walters walked towards him, syringe held ready. A sudden noise from behind him had Walters spinning, losing his balance and falling. The man with him went down under Tad's assault, quickly handcuffed and pulled to his feet and from the room.

Bill wrapped Cora in his arms and dodged out the back door, knowing he had to keep her safe. He had caught a glimpse of Lily and other officers behind Tad.

Finally, turning as he heard his name called, Bill cradled Cora against him as they sat on the bench on the back deck. Andrew sat down heavily in a chair across from them, a bandage now on his face.

"Andrew?" Bill's voice held the question he couldn't or wouldn't ask.

"I'm okay. They had taken out Terry and when I stopped to see if he was okay, that's when they got me. Not one of my better moments." He leaned back, his eyes sliding closed in fatigue. "Are you two okay?"

Cora spoke up. "I think we finally are, Andrew. Was that the last of them?"

Andrew nodded as he opened his eyes. "They were. We had everyone but Walters and everyone we had was eager to implicate him." He stared at the door, not quite sure how to word what he had to say. "He's dead. He fell on the syringe. Death was likely fairly quick. I think we can close Elizabeth's case now, Bill."

"I know we can. We're ready to move on." Bill studied Cora's face as she sat, deep in thought. "But what was Cora supposed to have, that they were sure she did and wanted to badly?"

"I have no idea. Do you, Cora?" Andrew's attention turned to Cora.

She looked up as she heard her name, bringing her thoughts back to the present. "There's a cave just outside of town, near the river. Have someone search it. That's the only place I can think of he may have left something. I had no idea Walters was involved." She shuddered at their close call.

"I don't think any of us did." Bill wrapped his arms tighter around her. "We've given our statements, Andrew. Anything else for tonight?"

Andrew stood. "No, my friend. Not tonight. I'm heading home myself. I need to hug my own wife. Catch you two later."

The activity finally died down in their home and Bill walked through it, checking all the doors and windows and setting the security system. He turned to find Cora standing watching him before she moved towards him.

"I thought I was going to lose you again, Bill." Her tears wet his flannel shirt.

"And I you. But God has been gracious, Cora. He's kept us alive and kept us hidden in the hollow of His hand. Just like He promised." He leaned back to look at her before claiming her mouth in a kiss. "Now that our adventure is over, what plans do we have for the weekend?"

"None. It's going to be one of those weekends where the doors stay locked and we don't answer to anyone or even answer our phones. We need time to just rest and relax and recuperate."

Arm around her as they headed back through the house, Bill dropped another kiss on her cheek. "I can handle a weekend like that."

Epilogue

Seven months later the trials were all over and the culprits had been sentenced. It had come out at the trials that Walters had been the main instigator of the drug trade, using his background as a chemist and science teacher to come up with the formulas. He had recruited unsuspecting teens to run the drugs for him. Anyone who got in his way ended up overdosing. Andrew had determined that Elizabeth had simply been in the wrong place at the wrong time and had seen something she wasn't supposed to see. Lock had fixated on Cora during their high school days. As had been thought, he hadn't planned to marry her at all, but had been ordered to by Walters, just in case she knew something. Cora had been right about where Lock had hidden documents that fully explained the drug trade that Walters had set up.

Cora turned one Saturday afternoon as she heard Bill's footsteps on the floor behind her. They were heading off to his brother's for his nephew's birthday party and were running late.

"All set?" Bill wrapped Cora in a hug. He had discovered, to his delight, that his bride loved to snuggle and cuddle.

"I am, but you're not."

"Five minutes. That's all I need." Bill hurried from the room as Cora shook her head.

She had news to share with him, that they would be starting their own family soon, but that could wait until later. She knew he would be thrilled.

Bill appeared behind her. "When are you going to tell me your news?"

She stared at him, a frown on her face. "What news?"

He tilted his head. "Cora!"

She grinned. "About work? I'm not going back to that. Instead, I'll be teaching at the college here."

"That's not your news. Spill."

She laughed at him, then sobered. "I have something to share." She shoved at him as he hugged her. "Listen, please. The proceeds from my travelogues will be going towards a foundation my editor has helped me set up, to help those who are trying to set up small businesses on their own. We called it the Elizabeth Buckley Foundation." She stopped speaking as she watched her husband, seeing the stunned look on his face and then the tears

"Thank you, Cora. She would like that." He hugged her tight again and just stood.

"Come on." She moved from him, heading for the door. "Wesley and Anna are waiting for us."

He shook his head as he gathered her close once more. "I'm glad about that, but that's not what I meant." He stared down at her until she nodded. "You are?"

"We are. Seven months or so to get used to the idea of being parents. Are we really ready for this?"

Bill kissed her, then hugged her tight. "We may not be, but God obviously thinks we are. We are blessed, darlin'. When I think of what we went through, how close we came to losing one another, we are indeed blessed."

Cora nodded, silent as her thoughts raced, her arms around her husband. A year previous she thought her life was over. Instead, God had bigger and better plans for both of them.

Dear Readers:

Thank you for picking up the story of Bill and Cora. Bill has been adamant over the course of a few months that he had a story to tell, and what a story! How many of us hide secrets from those around us, to keep a part of our lives so deep and personal we won't or can't talk about it? He needed a strong friend to compliment him, and I think Cora was just that person.

How many times have things happened to us, that we don't understand, or we don't see, or maybe we don't even know are happening, but God does and keeps us hidden in the hollow of His hand? That is a concept I have so loved since I was young, knowing that I am protected, no matter what happens to me or around me. God doesn't promise us an easy life, a pain-free life but what He promises is that He will never leave us or forsake us. He never ever fails to keep a promise.

God bless each one of you. Look for those moments, the God moments a pastor I know calls them. They are there. No matter where we are or who we're with, the moments are there that God blesses us with.

Sometimes, we're those God moments in someone else's life.

Ronna